This book should be returned to any branch of the
Lancashire County Library on or before the date shown

WOODS

BRELS
BURR
Cliff
EAT

Lancashire County Library
Bowran Street
Preston PR1 2UX

www.lancashire.gov.uk/libraries

LL1(A)

HOLLYWOOD HEAT

1950s Los Angeles: When six-year-old Daisy Adler vanishes from her upscale Hollywood Hills home, Detective Rusty Hallinan enters a case with more dangerous twists and turns than Mulholland Drive. Hallinan's life hits a bump or two of its own when he's dumped by his wife and falls for an enchanting young murder suspect half his age. But what's the connection between her murdered husband and a dying bar-room stripper? How does Hallinan's informant, exotic and endangered female impersonator Tyrisse Covington, fit into the puzzle? And where has little Daisy gone?

ARLETTE LEES

HOLLYWOOD HEAT

Complete and Unabridged

LINFORD
Leicester

First published in Great Britain

First Linford Edition
published 2016

A catalogue record for this book is available
from the British Library.

ISBN 978–1–4448–2700–2

Published by
F. A. Thorpe (Publishing)
Anstey, Leicestershire

Set by Words & Graphics Ltd.
Anstey, Leicestershire
Printed and bound in Great Britain by
T. J. International Ltd., Padstow, Cornwall

This book is printed on acid-free paper

118993637

1

Dark Rendezvous

Detective Rusty Hallinan sits nursing his third beer in a dark, smoky corner of the Alibi Room on Santa Monica Blvd. He is tall and solid and although he's sliding into his middle years, he carries his extra weight with a modicum of grace. He has a good Irish cop face, dark auburn hair and uncommonly bright blue eyes. Tonight he's in no mood to join the festivities and is equally unenthusiastic about going home to an empty house.

Dorothy left him a week ago. A make-up artist at MGM in Culver City, she often started her day early and worked late into the night. When shooting began on the set of *The Devil Wore Spurs* with newcomer Monty West, she started slipping in at dawn.

Monty was a Hollywood phenomenon. He'd been raised on a ranch and started out as a stuntman, but his good looks and charismatic personality catapulted him into starring roles almost overnight. When Hallinan asked Dorothy if there was anything she needed to tell him, she responded by packing a suitcase and moving in with West, fifteen years her junior.

Eleven years of matrimony, and he'd always been someone the guys at the station looked up to. He didn't cheat on his wife or his taxes. He was generous with money and took Dorothy to dinner at nice restaurants. He didn't know where things had gone off the rails or what he could have done to prevent it. He blamed it on the miscarriage she'd had soon after they'd married, but that seemed like such a long time ago. Nevertheless, it stood between them like a big white elephant they pretended not to see.

New Year's Eve is not suited for quiet contemplation. The noise level is brain-numbing as midnight approaches. Voices compete with the cha-chunk of cigarette packs tumbling into the tray of the machine, dice cups slapping against the bar, and a bubbling Worlitzer whose songs are drowned out by the ambient revelry.

A beautiful woman with hips as tight as a sailor's knot walks toward him through a shimmering veil of smoke. Her slender form is poured into a form-fitting gown of sapphire satin. Earrings the size of pie plates glitter from her ears. A plastic pin, looking very out of place on her glamorous dress, reads: GIVE TO ST. MARTHA'S SOUP KITCHEN.

'Hi, sugar.' Her voice has the texture of rough velvet, smoky and deep. Hallinan is tempted to look behind him to see who she's talking to, except his chair is pressed against the back wall. She leans over his table, her cigarette trailing a ribbon of silver smoke. For a moment he forgets about his empty house, his unfaithful wife and the young actor she's sleeping with.

The candle in the ruby glass ball on the table illuminates elegant cheekbones and sculpted features. The woman is ethnically ambiguous, with a light caramel complexion and almond-shaped hazel eyes. She could cross the color line from either direction without raising an eyebrow and probably does.

'You don't know who I am, do you,

darling?' she says.

Hallinan takes a closer look. Cops have excellent recall when it comes to faces, but he can't put this elegant creature in context. Despite her feminine allure he picks up on a few anomalies — knuckles the size of small walnuts . . . a slightly prominent Adam's apple.

'Holy geezus, Tyrone!' says Hallinan with a jolt of recognition. 'You almost gave me a heart attack. What are you doing masquerading around town like that?' Ty is a high-end female impersonator, the best in the business. He receives top billing in an always-crowded club called Dark Desires in South Central L.A. Until tonight Hallinan has never seen him, or her — yes, 'her' seems more appropriate — in full theatrical regalia.

The problem is, masquerading in 1950s Los Angeles is a crime. Ordinance 5022, passed in 1898, makes it illegal to dress in the attire of a sex other than one's own. It is punishable by a five-hundred-dollar fine and six months in jail. The law is designed to target people who are not a conventional fit by the mores and prejudices of

4

the time — cross-dressers, transvestites and others who might be considered too light of foot or fluttery of wrist. As far as Hallinan is concerned, Ty can dress up like a Christmas tree. Ty is Hallinan's most effective and trusted informant, leading to the arrest and incarceration of any number of dangerous offenders, especially those who prey on children.

But here's the mystery. Two years ago Ty was a respected drama and math teacher at Hollywood High School. There were those who might have suspected that he wasn't as straight as the road to Vegas, but he was well-liked by staff and students and had only six months to go before he achieved tenure. Then, without explanation, he was gone . . . fired. After that he bloomed into a rare hothouse flower.

'I stepped through the looking glass,' says Ty, pressing a false eyelash in place. 'And it's Miss Tyrisse from now on, darling — not to be mistaken for Tyrone, who went to live with his maiden aunt in Pasadena.'

Hallinan laughs and lights a Chesterfield. 'Okay, Miss Tyrisse it is.'

'There's a lot of money floating around on New Year's Eve,' she says. 'It's a good time to collect for the soup kitchen at the church. I like to stand by the cigarette machine when people have their wallets out. You carrying your wallet tonight, Rusty?'

Hallinan smiles, pulls a ten from his wallet and hands it to her. She puts it in a velvet bag with a cross embroidered on the front and slips it into her beaded evening purse.

'Thank you, darling. You're an angel.'

Hallinan leans back in his chair and melts into the shadows until the only thing visible is the hot red eye of his cigarette. 'You said you were going to bring me Lobo Calderone. What's going on with that?'

'Listen Rusty, the guy's a ghost. He drifts from one fleabag hotel to another. I hear he's holding a young woman against her will. Poor little thing thought she got off the bus in the Emerald City. Trouble is, the man behind the curtain isn't making her Hollywood dream come true. I don't know her name, but he calls her Cupcake.'

'That's a good start. Just keep on it. You bring me Calderone and I'll make it worth your while.' Hallinan blows a stream of smoke to the side. 'You still in the apartment on Cheremoya?'

'That tenancy ended abruptly, like my position at the high school. Now I'm at the Empire on Vermont. Room 320.' The Empire Hotel is neither the best nor the worst address in town, but it's certainly a couple of pegs down from Cheremoya.

'Sit down. Tell me what's behind all this bad luck?'

Tyrisse slips gracefully into the chair across from Hallinan, then leans across the table until they're almost cheek to cheek. She's about to say something when the door opens and Buzz Storch from undercover vice blows in off the street. Ty tenses and shrinks back in her chair.

Buzz wears a dark nylon jacket and a black knit cap pulled low on his forehead. He taps his fingers on the bar and waits for Red Dooley to finish tossing coins in the cash drawer. At five feet five inches, Storch barely makes the department's minimum height requirement, although he overcompensates by taking on the muscle and temperament of a junkyard dog.

Hallinan and proprietor Red Dooley have a history going back to high school at St. Francis Academy. After graduation, Dooley followed his old man into the bar business and Hallinan followed his onto the Force . . . two apples who didn't fall far from the family tree.

'This is my cue to head out the back door,' whispers Ty.

'Stay right where you are,' says Hallinan. In the shifting light from the candle he notices swelling on Ty's cheekbone and a purple bruise on her throat. Hallinan nods his head toward Storch. 'He do that?'

'Three nights ago, me and some of the girls from Dark Desires were sitting in Willie's Donut Shop after our act . . . you know, the all-night place on Main. A couple of goons from vice busted in and slapped us around for congregating. Storch worked me over a little in the alley, but when he started to take off his belt with that big buckle, the cook

8

stepped out the back door of the cafeteria and Storch stomped off. He looked over his shoulder and said, 'Catch you later, sweetheart.' With Storch you never know what's coming next. A bullet in the head? A throw-down in your hand? We ladies aren't exactly the darlings of L.A. vice.'

In the current political and judicial climate, people like Ty are easy prey. It's open season on anyone who's a little different or openly bucks convention. Under Chief William Parker, incidents of harassment and brutality go undocumented by police and unreported by the press. Los Angeles is all glitz and glamour unless you turn it over and examine its dark underbelly.

Red hands Storch an envelope that he stuffs inside his jacket. 'He's coming our way,' says Hallinan, crushing his cigarette in the ashtray. 'Sit tight. I'll handle it.'

'How's it hanging?' says Storch, approaching their table with a swagger. He has a bulldog face with a serious underbite.

'We're a little busy here, Storch.'

'Don't tell me this thing is your informant,' he says, bumping the back of

Ty's chair with his knee. Hallinan sees every muscle in Ty's body clench.

'Don't do that,' says Hallinan, energy building in his right hand.

'What? I'm just making conversation. It's New Year's Eve.'

'Okay, let's converse about the envelope inside your jacket. You hitting Red up to cover your third ex-wife's alimony? Three strikes and you're out. Isn't that the way it goes in matrimonial circles?'

'You're a jerk, you know that, Hallinan?' He pivots, his elbow just missing Ty's head. He marches across the room and out the door.

'He's not going to forget this,' says Ty. Her hand trembles and she puts out her cigarette.

'Neither am I.'

'He'll be waiting for me in the parking lot. There's stuff about this guy you can't even imagine.'

'You mean he's not the violent moron I think he is?' That gets a shaky smile. 'Come on. I'll see you home.'

They walk down the sidewalk to the parking lot. Storch's car is gone, but the exhaust still hangs in the air. Hallinan and Ty climb into their respective cars. The Empire is a ten-minute drive in medium traffic. He escorts her to the recessed entry. 'You're holding something back.'

'I'll tell you when the time is right.'

Storch's car drifts slowly past the hotel with the lights out. He parks in a palm grove down the street and watches them from the shadows.

Tyrisse gets into the elevator. When Hallinan turns around, the Studebaker is gone.

★　★　★

Hallinan's new Buick hums west on Hollywood Blvd., reflections rippling over the polished chrome. He pulls to the curb in front of the Pantages Theater. Mobster Johnny Stompanato steps out of the Frolic Room next door with Lana Turner on his arm. He has golden Sicilian skin and the perfect proportions of an underwear model. Lana moves in a cloud of white fox fur as they climb into a waiting limousine and go north toward the hills. A notorious

11

movie mogul told Dorothy that the pair had explosive chemistry, the kind that's capable of blowing up the science lab or bringing down the studio.

Hallinan gets out of the car and limps across the sidewalk, his bum knee a souvenir from a Jap grenade on the Island of Luzon. The poster in the display case reads:

WHILE THE CITY SLEEPS

A foolish Girl . . . A dangerous Boy . . . A fatal Moment.

Just his kind of movie. He buys a ticket and goes inside. It's a cavernous Egyptian palace, hushed by acres of deep plush carpets, a steep balcony and luxurious lounges in the restrooms. Half an hour into the movie his box of popcorn tumbles to the floor. The man in the seat behind him kicks the back of his chair and tells him to stop snoring.

Hallinan parks at the curb in front of his house on Sandalwood Street at 2 a.m. It's a quiet older neighborhood where roots of mature trees capsize the sidewalks and few residents lock their houses or cars. His house is a brown-shingled two-story with an orange tree, garden plot and clothesline out back and a soon-to-be-banned incinerator near the rear fence.

He always parks on the street because the one-car garage with alley access is filled with fishing gear. He used to dream of fishing trips to Lake Almanor with his children, but his marriage had gone cold and the children never happened and he'd drifted childless into middle age.

When he steps onto the front porch the silence makes him pause. Something isn't quite right. His Chihuahua, Beelzebub — 'Beezer' for short — should be squealing and prancing, his nose pressed to the windowpane. He enters the living room and snaps on the light. The only sound is the hum of the fridge and a clank from the basement furnace.

He walks through the house to the back yard. He whistles and calls the dog's name. After looking around the neighborhood without success, he goes back in the house. In the den he finds his bottom desk drawer pried open, a screwdriver on the desktop. His framed commendation for bravery is on the floor, the glass broken, a lady's shoe print stamped on the face of the document.

Dorothy!

★ ★ ★

Los Angeles is the most populous county in the United States, all 4,752 squares miles of city, mountain, desert and seashore. Only one county is larger and it's in California too — San Bernardino, at 20,105 square miles, the largest in the United States.

There's another Los Angeles, the one you don't see on the fancy brochures with their colorful displays of palm trees, movie stars' houses and the Hollywood sign above Beechwood Canyon. It's the one just east of the L.A. River, the one that's swept under the rug so to speak. If you live in Hollywood, Culver City or Beverly Hills you've probably never been there. You'll never see overpasses scribbled with graffiti or young toughs tattooed with gang insignia. But, don't get me wrong. That doesn't mean that upscale L.A. doesn't have its secret vices. It has exotic vices you never knew existed and the money to pay for them. They're simply indulged in glass houses set like jewels in the Hollywood Hills or in Spanish mansions behind high walls and impenetrable hedges.

In that other world, east of the Los Angeles River, at the dead-end of an unpaved road, is Club Velvet. It's a strip joint hidden away in an area called Boyle Heights, between the housing projects and the freight yard. It's where men come to drink and gamble and indulge their darker addictions. It's not that easy to find unless you know it's there, and all the wrong people do. Club Velvet is where pretty young Crystal Monet took the first wrong turn in her life's short journey.

'I want you on stage in two minutes,' says Cesar, looming over the shivering girl on the dressing-room couch. He's dressed in black, silver conchos flashing from his western hat. Tall and hard, the only thing that separates him from movie star good looks is a face as acne-scarred as a bad cement pour.

'I'm not well, Cesar. Please, put Ariceli

on, just for tonight,' she begs.

'You're the one they pay to see,' he says, pulling her up by her long blonde hair. A few strands tangle in his turquoise ring and she cries out as he rips his hand free.

Crystal was just out of high school when Cesar offered her 'easy money' to strip at the club over the summer. She needed tuition for nursing school in the fall and money to send home to her mother, who'd grown too fat to fit behind the steering wheel of a car.

'It's time you earn your keep,' her mother snapped. 'Cesar is a friend of your cousin's. Give the man what he wants.'

With great misgivings, she cleaned out her closet and moved into the back room at Club Velvet. At least there was one less mouth to feed in a family with six kids, no father and a mother who walked with the help of two canes.

Crystal turned out to be Cesar's big money-maker. When summer was over and she had the money for school, he refused to let her go. Her attempt at escape resulted in a sprained shoulder and cracked rib. After that, he withheld her wages and sometimes her tips.

Cesar pulls Crystal's costume from the rack and throws it at her. It consists of big fluffy ostrich feathers, a handful of chiffon and pink velvet gloves.

'Put it on and get out there. Now!'

She can hear the customers stomping their feet and calling her name. 'Crystal, Crystal, Crystal!'

'I can't. I'm not well.'

'What is that supposed to mean?'

'I'm sick to my stomach every morning like before. I asked you to stay away from me.'

His face hardens, like it's all her fault, like everything that goes wrong in his life is because of her. 'I'll set you up one last time, but don't let it happen again.'

'I want to go home to my mother.' She starts to cry. 'I can't go through this again.'

He leans an inch from her face. 'You'll do exactly as I say.'

The next day a bus carries Crystal to an abandoned building near Skid Row. Alone and scared, she walks the three flights to a room where plaster crumbles from the walls and wind blows through a broken window. The same withered crone who fixed her up the last time snatches the two hundred dollars as soon as she walks through the door. She was a surgical nurse in a previous incarnation, or so Crystal had been told. The nameless woman dumps a bag of surgical instruments on a TV tray beside an old kitchen table.

'You know the routine. Get undressed and get on the table,' says the woman. 'I don't have all day.'

The examination is over almost as soon as it begins.

'Get dressed,' says the nurse, tossing the instruments in her cracked leather bag.

'But you haven't done anything.'

'I can't help you.'

Crystal sits up and wraps her arms around her shivering body. 'What do you mean?'

'You're not pregnant.'

'That's impossible! I feel just like I did the last time.'

The nurse looks at her through the hound-dog wrinkles around her eyes. 'You need to see a physician, dearie — a real doctor. Something's not right in there.'

'Like what? What do you mean?'

'I don't know, but it's not good.'

Crystal gets off the table and hurries into her clothes. 'Cesar's going to want his money back,' she says.

'I charge for my time, missy.' The hunched crone picks up her bag, clatters down the stairs and jumps in a taxi, leaving Crystal standing alone in the center of the room.

★ ★ ★

New Year's Eve, December 31, 1956.

Up-and-coming young architect Gavin Chase is turned around in the barrios of Boyle Heights. Not quite midnight, and firecrackers are exploding in rusty barrels adjacent to the freight yard. A pipe bomb blows down a fence. A shotgun blasts skyward, raining buckshot down on Gavin's car. He feels a familiar stitch of pain in his right side, made more painful by the stress

19

of being so completely out of his element. The wind is up, electrical wires whipping between the utility poles.

In late October Gavin met a drop-dead blonde at a medical clinic in the Wilshire district. She was stranded with neither car nor bus fare. Her vulnerability broke through his defenses faster than a burglar picks a lock and they ended up in a motel room on Western Blvd. He gave her money and she took it, but mostly she wanted to talk about her situation at Club Velvet. Maybe with his help she'd eventually find the courage to leave, but she'd never be able to do it alone.

That's how it began — a one-night stand, something reckless and impulsive, something he'd never done in his six years of marriage. Even as he swore not to see Crystal again, the hormonal pull was too strong to resist. She was a delicious confection, sweet and yielding ... and lost. That didn't mean he was in love with her in the 'forever' way he loved Amanda. Now, on the cusp of a new year, he'd grown tired of pushing his luck. Tonight he'd pick Crystal up at a pre-arranged location, take her to a safe house for battered women and get back to his real life.

A group of teenagers in a low-rider toss an empty beer can against the windshield of his station wagon, then peel into the night. He passes street-corner bodegas, store-front churches, second-hand shops, and a Rescue Mission with a gold neon cross burning a hole in the darkness.

Gavin swoops beneath a graffitied overpass. When he comes out the other end the street lights are gone from his rearview mirror. Weeds grow in the cracks of sidewalks and everything except bars and liquor stores are closed for the night. He can't wait to get back to his clean, safe world at the foot of the Hollywood Hills.

He pulls to the side of the road, snaps on the roof light and unfolds his map. He glances nervously at his watch. By now he should be on his way home. Amanda will be dressed for the party, restlessly tapping her toe.

He folds the map, pulls back into the street and passes a noisy cantina on his left, its cracked stucco walls painted coral and turquoise, like a ride at the Beach Boardwalk. Out front a knot of men smoke fat joints, their eyes hidden by smoke and shadows beneath cocked fedoras, gold watch chains dangling from the vests of their zoot suits. Suspicious glances cut in his direction, their wariness met with equal unease.

A mile further and a deserted gas station appears on his right. He pulls beside two battered 1920 gas pumps and lets the engine idle. A rusty motor oil sign flaps against the wall of the dark auto repair bay. Wind rocks the car and dead leaves cartwheel across the hood. Crystal is nowhere in sight.

A man appears at his window. Where the hell had he come from? He wears a black hat and taps on the glass with a big blue ring. Tension causes the pain in his side to ratchet up a notch.

The stranger has a pencil-thin mustache reminiscent of a silent-film Casanova, his black eyes set close to the bridge of an aquiline nose, thin lips drawn back in what might pass for a smile in a friendlier setting.

'I have a message from . . . ' The wind blows away the words.

'What?' says Gavin, rolling down the window. A gun appears out of nowhere. 'Is this a joke?' Gavin breaks a sweat. He wants to unbutton his coat and loosen his tie. He tries to punch the gas pedal, but his foot freezes. 'Here, you want my wallet?'

The man doesn't answer, his black eyes swallowing the light.

Gavin's mind is spinning, sweat prickling like flea bites on his scalp. He doesn't want to give up the money, but he has to get the gun out of his face. What will he tell Amanda when he comes home with an empty wallet? He's never lied to her before . . . until recently.

The wallet is half out of his pocket when a bullet whispers into Gavin's left temple. There's no time to contemplate his fate, or speak Amanda's name one last time. He couldn't be deader if the Saturday-night special had been a bazooka. Across the street a man walking his dog pauses, glances over, then continues down the dark sidewalk.

The gunman pockets the weapon and takes the wallet from the dead man's hand. He smiles. It's stuffed with cash, as if the poor sucker had paid for his own hit.

2

The Night Has Eyes

In 212 of the upscale Castleton Apartments, Amanda Chase steps from her bubble bath. She's young and petite, with intelligent blue-green eyes and a secret she's saving for Gavin at tonight's New Year's Eve party. After six years of marriage she's two months pregnant with their first child.

She runs her fingers over the new party dress that lies across the bedspread and smiles at her good fortune. She enjoys a happy marriage to a husband whose star is rising in architectural circles. They'd put a down payment down on an old Spanish house in Topanga Canyon and are signing the closing papers in two weeks.

After a sprinkling of talcum powder, Amanda slips into lacy white underthings and shimmery silk stockings. She stands in front of the dressing-table mirror, sweeps her golden-brown hair into a rhinestone clip, then sits on the edge of the bed and pulls on sparkly high-heeled shoes. A touch of lipstick, a whisper of perfume, and she's set. She glances at her watch. Gavin should be here by now.

Dack Traynor stands in the windy darkness outside Amanda's bedroom window, his camera aimed through a tiny crack at the edge of the curtain. Gavin had once caught him peeping and gone into a testosterone-fueled rage that scared the bejesus out of him. Even a bloodless stuffed shirt like Gavin can get pretty riled when it comes to his beautiful young wife.

Amanda looks in the mirror and tucks a stray wisp of hair behind her ear; then, as if a spider had crawled across her skin, she touches the back of her neck. With a twinge of apprehension she walks across the carpet to the window.

Dack steps away from the glass with a mischievous grin and presses his back against the building so he can't be seen. Amanda separates the curtains, allowing a golden slice of light to cut across the second-story walkway. He holds his breath until the curtain drops, then makes a dash for 214. By the time Amanda opens the front door he's safely inside his apartment. Dack's wife Gail looks up from her book. She has sharp eyes and a razor-cut bob like the wealthy women who come to her teller window at the bank.

'What are you doing with the camera?'

'I didn't want to leave it in the car overnight. Want to go to the Carnival Room?' he says, setting the camera on top of the bookcase.

'I think I'll stick with my book. There are too many drunks on the road tonight.'

Just what he wants to hear.

Dack scrapes a match to life on the sole of his shoe and lights a cigarette. Standing there in his button-fly jeans, a dark curl falling over his forehead, he looks much the same as he did twelve years ago when she'd fallen for him in high school. He still exudes the same sensory cocktail of cigarette smoke and overactive hormones she once found so appealing.

Dack can't hold a job. He hasn't paid a bill since her promotion. He sneaks money from her purse like a schoolboy and runs up her credit cards. He's incapable of fidelity and inept at covering his tracks.

Every day at the bank Gail meets nice men who are doing productive things with their lives. Some of them are single. Some of them would like to take her out.

Beneath her probing gaze, Dack shifts his weight to the other hip. 'Why are you looking at me like that?' he says.

'You'd better not be up to your old tricks, Dack. One more misstep and you're on your own.'

'I'm going out,' he says, rolling his shoulders and cracking tension from his neck. 'The quiet around here is deafening.'

* * *

Dr. Nathan Adler, Plastic Surgeon To The Stars, is celebrating his 50th birthday. His wife Helen is combining his celebration with their annual New Year's Eve party. A man of pedestrian looks and extraordinary skill, he is the closest thing his illustrious clientele have to the Fountain of Youth.

Tonight, lights and laughter pour from the party onto the balconies of the last house at the summit of Fairbanks Drive in the Hollywood Hills. The pink Mediterranean is stacked like giant's blocks above the three-car garage at street level, the wrought-iron gate opening onto stairs leading up to the front door.

The Hollywood sign is visible across a sweep of canyon slightly above and to the left of the address, and the wild expanse of Griffith Park abuts the property to the north and east. On this last night of the year the house looks like a festive wedding cake ablaze with a million candles.

The celebration is a catered affair with plenty of food. Hors d'oeuvres and champagne circulate on silver platters. There are balloons and crêpe-paper streamers and a library table set with beautifully wrapped and ribboned gifts. Nathan's white-haired Aunt Sarah has prepared a special table set with kosher delicacies for the observant among them.

Ladies dressed in their finest furs and jewels talk about upcoming movie roles, trips abroad and the latest styles; the gentlemen about their latest deals, theatrical and otherwise. Young talent chats up casting directors, while the directors wonder how far the hopefuls will go to get the parts they so passionately covet. In short, it's your typical Hollywood party.

Nathan's wife Helen, a slender, greying blonde with a diamond on her finger the size of a bicycle reflector, sits on a brocade sofa chatting with Lana Turner and her stunningly handsome escort. It's rumored that Helen suffers migraines, the biggest of whom is her husband Nathan.

Trudy Shawn, hot off a starring role in a Broadway musical, is a perky red-head in a yellow flapper dress, long rope of pearls and a feathered headband. She's come with her agent, the stately switch-hitter Todd Sinclair, resplendent in tux and tails.

Trudy gives Todd a friendly jab in the ribs with her elbow. 'Look at the gorgeous hunk with Turner.' She watches him snap a flame from his monogrammed lighter and touch the tip to Lana's cigarette. 'God, if he was more beautiful, he'd be a woman.'

'That's Johnny Stompanato, Mickey Cohen's bodyguard and bagman.'

She makes a soft growling noise. 'He can guard my body anytime.'

Todd flutters a wrist adorned with a very expensive watch. 'My sentiments exactly.'

Trudy twists a bouncy curl around her finger and rubs an ice cube from her drink against her throat. 'My radiator's boiling over.'

'Then you might consider putting that ice between your knees,' he says. She sputters a laugh and nearly chokes on her champagne. There's the murmur of voices as a small child, rubbing a sleepy eye, comes down the carpeted staircase from the second level.

'Oh look, Todd, isn't she adorable?'

A golden-haired, blue-eyed little girl of five or six stands at the bottom of the stairs in a long white nightgown with strawberry appliqué at the neckline.

'That's Daisy Adler, the little princess of the house. She has a career modeling kiddie clothes for the leading designers,' says Todd.

'Nothing like getting a jump on your career,' says Trudy. 'My mother didn't push me onto the stage until I was seven.'

Daisy trots sleepily across the room and puts her head in Helen's lap. She smiles and tousles the child's curls, a softness illuminating her features.

'Helen and Nathan tried for years to have children but his sperm are lazy swimmers,' says Todd conspiratorially. 'They took some time away and returned with a newborn after he'd undergone some revolutionary new treatment.'

Helen gives Daisy a hug. 'Back to bed, darling.'

'I can't sleep without Teddy, Mom.'

'Cats like the full moon. He'll be back tomorrow.'

Johnny reaches in his pocket and peels a bill from his fat roll of cash. 'Here, *cara mia*, go put this in your piggy bank.'

'Thank you, Uncle Johnny,' say Daisy, giving him a peck on the cheek.

'Johnny, a ten is far too much!' says Helen. 'She's just a baby.'

'You're right. Next time I'll make it two fives.'

Lana laughs. 'Helen, you know he's incorrigible.'

'Off you go,' says Helen. 'Have Sigrid tuck you in.' Daisy toddles back up the stairs.

A flashbulb explodes inches from Lana's face. She gasps and shelters her eyes from the blinding flash. Johnny shoots out of his seat and grabs the front of the photographer's shirt with an iron fist. The man holding the camera is in his thirties with white-blond slicked-back hair and the effete air of a character lifted from a Fitzgerald novel.

'I ought to shove that camera down your throat,' says Johnny.

'Is that a threat? Did you hear that, Helen? It was definitely a threat.'

'Please, sit down,' says Lana, tugging on Johnny's sleeve. 'I'm perfectly fine. He simply caught me off guard.'

'Do go away and let us be, Horst,' says Helen. Horst puts a bored look on his face, tosses his head and drifts into the crowd. Johnny sits back down, still fuming.

'That was interesting,' says Trudy from across the room. 'By the way, where's the birthday boy hiding out? I haven't seen him for ages.'

'You see the Swedish au pair?'

'The what?'

'Sigrid Nordgren, the tall teenager with the braid over her shoulder.'

'Oh, don't tell me it's going to be that kind of evening.' A series of flashbulbs pop in rapid succession. 'Oh god, it's that insufferable man with the camera and he's looking our way.'

'That's Horst Kepler, Photographer To The Stars,' says Todd. 'Every celebrity who's anybody has a Kepler hanging above his fireplace. He turned Daisy Adler into an overnight sensation, but I wouldn't trust him as far as I can throw him.'

'What do you mean?'

'One of my clients says the guy has a dark side, but wouldn't elaborate. If I were Helen, I wouldn't leave Daisy alone with him, but you didn't hear that from me. Let's escape while he's changing film.'

Todd tosses Trudy's Marabou cape over her shoulders and they step through the French doors onto the front balcony. He shelters two cigarettes from the wind and lights them with his Zippo. They smoke in silence, looking at the moon and the swirl of icy stars floating above Mt. Lee.

'What's that odd noise?' says Trudy, looking toward the hills.

'Don't you have coyotes in New York?'

She gives him a quizzical look, wind ruffling her short curls. 'Not in Times Square, darling.'

'They're making love to the moon.'

The grandfather clock in the foyer strikes midnight and cheers go up from inside the house. There's the rattle of noise-makers, the sound of plastic horns and the pop, pop, pop of flashbulbs.

'Happy New Year, Trudy,' he says and kisses her on the forehead. 'Welcome to Hollywood.'

'Happy New Year, handsome.'

Down the street three dark shadows lope quietly through the neighborhood. A garbage can topples over, the lid rolling into a bed of ice plant. A neighbor whistles her Pekingese into the house and quickly shuts the door.

* * *

The phone rings and Amanda rushes to answer it. 'Gavin!' she says.

'No, dear, this is Julia Kravitz. It's eleven thirty and everyone is wondering where you are.'

'Gavin ran an errand and he's not back yet. I'm worried.'

'An errand at this hour? There's another name for that, honey, and she's probably blonde and hot to trot.'

'Oh Julia,' she laughs. 'You know Gavin's not like that.'

'Neither were my three exes until I hired a private detective to monitor their extracurricular activities. I wouldn't put my money on George here, either.' She giggles. 'George, stop that! You'll make me drop the phone. Amanda, dear, if you can't make the party call me tomorrow. We'll do lunch later in the week.'

When the clock strikes midnight, Amanda steps out of her new shoes. She removes the rhinestone clip and her hair tumbles in soft waves around her shoulders. Cheers go up from the party in the apartment two doors down. Plastic whistles and paper horns cut through the stillness.

Amanda walks to the window. Confetti floats over the second-story railing like silver snowflakes, and a trio of balloons floats over the rooftops. She looks into the darkness and whispers Gavin's name.

* * *

Rusty is sweeping up the broken glass in the den when the phone rings.

'I've been trying to reach you all night,' says Dorothy.

'I went to a movie.'

'Oh please, I can smell the beer on your breath from here.'

'It's late and I'm tired. What do you want?'

'I'm coming by in the morning. There are some papers I need signed.'

'Looks like you've already been here.'

'Oh that. I bumped the commendation off the wall and didn't have time to clean up the mess. It shouldn't be hard to find another frame.'

'Get to the point, Dorothy. What kind of papers are you talking about?'

'It's too complicated to go into on the phone.'

'You broke into my desk. You left a nasty gouge in the wood.'

'I needed copies of last year's IRS filing,' she says.

'The next time, call before you come. I don't need my house ransacked.'

'I am calling.'

'I'm sleeping in tomorrow, so I don't want you showing up before ten. And Dorothy, I want my dog back.'

'If I leave Beezer with you, he's alone all day. I bring him on the set where he gets a lot of attention.'

'I want my dog.'

'And people in hell want ice-water. Besides, what makes him yours?'

'You gave him to me for my forty-third birthday, remember?'

'I have no recollection of that event.'

A loaded silence follows as Hallinan takes a deep breath and lets it out slowly. 'When are you coming home, Dorothy? I don't know what point you're trying to make, but I think you've made it.'

'Please don't do this, Rusty.'

'Haven't I always been good to you? I don't understand where all this hostility is coming from.'

'Of course you don't,' she says and hangs up.

By two a.m. Rusty has showered and hit the sack. He has one more day of vacation before he's back on the roster and he plans to make the most of it by turning on the TV, putting his feet up and eating a half gallon of chocolate ice cream.

By three a.m., his grand plan has gone up in smoke.

3

Missing

Nathan finally comes downstairs and opens his gifts. There's an elegant gold wristwatch, bottles of vintage wine, a first edition of *Tropic of Cancer*, a new set of golf clubs, and gift certificates to the finest purveyors of gentlemen's attire in Beverly Hills. Once he's thanked his guests for their generosity, the caterers pack up and the party thins out.

Several people are still milling around when Helen goes upstairs. Even though she's had very little to drink, she feels weak by the time she reaches the landing on the second floor. She removes her jewelry at the dressing table and walks down the hall to Daisy's room.

A full moon shines through the French door that opens onto the patio separating the back of the house from the upslope of the mountain. Through a connecting door on the right wall of the nursery is Sigrid's room. When she crosses the pink carpet and bends beneath the ruffle-topped canopy of Daisy's bed, she senses something isn't quite right. She snaps on the lamp. The bed is empty. She taps lightly and opens Sigrid's door, expecting to find the two curled up together as they often are.

'Sigrid, are you awake?' she whispers. There is no response. She flicks the light switch. The bed is empty. She checks Daisy's bathroom and walk-in closet. She turns on the bug light and looks out the French door. The wind is up and the moon hangs like a Chinese lantern above the hills.

As Helen steps into the hall, Sigrid walks toward her from the opposite direction, her face flushed, a strand of hair escaping from the thick russet braid over her shoulder.

'Are you looking for me, Mrs. Adler?'

'I'm looking for Daisy. She's not in her room.'

'I tucked her in hours ago.'

'Is there a problem?' asks Nathan,

41

stepping from his den. He smoothes his thinning hair with the palm of his hand and straightens his tie. The gesture does not go unnoticed.

'I can't find Daisy,' she says.

Word spreads quickly. Johnny and Lana help search the house, while Trudy and Todd check the street out front.

'She can't go far in her nightgown,' says Aunt Sarah, fingering her coral necklace. 'It's terribly cold out there.'

Nathan goes to the phone and calls L.A.P.D. The moment he asks the remaining guests not to leave, the seriousness of the situation sinks in. If Daisy isn't found quickly, the news will hit the front page of the *Examiner* like a gallon of red paint.

Men who've attended the gathering with women other than their wives stumble over one another to get out the door. An older married man and a youthful blonde actor whom he supports on the side give one another a look of glitter-eyed panic and race to separate cars.

Horst Kepler on the other hand is having the time of his life, gleefully snapping photo after photo of the fleeing

42

guests until his supply of film is exhausted. He rushes to the foyer, sweeps the guest book from its pedestal and bolts for the door.

'I'll take that, young man,' says Sarah, rushing over, her voice crackling with indignation. Horst punts her aside and flees like a delinquent who's keyed the principal's car.

'That rotten swine!' she says. 'This is intolerable.'

Helen leads a small group of close friends to Daisy's room. She opens the French door and steps onto the patio. A chilly wind whips the soft golden fabric of her gown. Another step and her toe hits the corner of Teddy's food dish. It's turned upside-down and the water bowl is empty. She turns toward Sigrid.

'What are the cat's things doing out here? Haven't I told you that we feed Teddy in the kitchen? And why is Daisy's patio door unlocked?'

'I was trying to coax Teddy inside with food. I left the door unlocked so Daisy could let him in.'

Johnny is first to see the muddy canine

tracks circling the water bowl. He shoots Nathan a cautionary look, but it's too late.

'Oh my God!' says Helen. 'A coyote's been back here.'

'Calm down, Mrs. Adler,' says Sigrid. 'They're probably tracks from the neighbor's dog.'

Helen spins around and gives Sigrid a resounding slap in the face that sends her staggering sideways. 'Don't you dare tell me to calm down, you deceitful little trollop.'

Dead silence. No one has ever seen Helen lose her temper. Lana squeezes Johnny's arm. 'I think we should go,' she says. 'This is clearly a matter for L.A.P.D.'

Helen takes a step toward Sigrid. The girl takes a step back, pressing a hand to her cheek. 'We pay you good money and ask very little in return,' says Helen quietly. 'Where were you when you were supposed to be watching my baby? Answer me. Where were you?' Sigrid's pale blue eyes simmer with loathing.

'Exactly where you think I was . . . Helen.'

The color drains from Nathan's face.

He reaches out a comforting hand to his wife and a consoling look to Sigrid.

'Don't touch me,' says Helen with frightening calm. 'Stay away from me. Both of you.'

* * *

Dorothy's phone call has left Hallinan staring at the ceiling with adrenaline coursing through his blood. He'd just begun to doze when the phone rings. He moans and pulls the pillow over his head, but the ringing doesn't stop. A sliver of moonlight slips beneath the window shade and shadows of tree branches loop across the bedspread. The luminous dial on the clock reads 3 a.m. Hallinan reaches over and grabs the phone, knocking an ashtray to the floor.

'What?' he grumbles into the receiver.

'Rusty, it's Tug.' Tug being Sergeant Thomas 'Tug' Boatwright, his partner in Missing Persons Detail. 'I hope you're not sleeping.'

'That's the dumbest thing you've ever said.' Hallinan swings his legs over the edge of the bed and turns on the lamp.

He squints against the glare and tosses a T-shirt over the shade as he fumbles for a cigarette and match.

'Captain Stanek has a case for us.'

'Now? I'm not due back until the second. Do you know how long I've waited for a few days off?'

'He says it's important. Ever hear the name Nathan Adler? Dr. Nathan Adler?'

'Dorothy's mentioned him. Is he missing?'

'His six-year-old daughter vanished during a house party tonight. The captain has assigned you to lead on the case. Sergeants Garner and Strongbow are up there now.'

As Tug fills him in, Hallinan is pulling clothes out of the closet, dragging the phone along by the extension cord. 'I thought Edwards and Conover were next up?'

'This one is too high-profile. The captain doesn't want them leaking their guts to the tabloids again.'

'What's the address?'

'How about I pick you up on the way? Parking's at a premium up there.'

Hallinan finishes the cold coffee in last

night's pot. Fifteen minutes later they're driving into the hills.

*   *   *

At 3:15 a.m. Amanda calls Hollywood Station. Sergeant Dunnigan is on the desk. The phones have been ringing off the hook all night, most of the calls concerning bar fights, traffic mishaps and errant spouses. Amanda gets his standard response.

'Believe me, Mrs. Chase, by morning your husband will be home with an empty wallet and a head as big as a cabbage.'

'No disrespect, Sergeant, but it is morning. Something has gone terribly wrong.'

'If your husband hasn't returned in 48 hours, come to the station, file a Missing Persons Report and I'll jump on it like a crow on a June-bug.'

*   *   *

On the east side of town four teenaged boys and a girl with haystack hair see a car parked by the old gas station. They pull their stolen pickup alongside the station wagon and kill the headlights. Fanta runs over to check it out.

'There's a drunk passed out in here, Benito,' she says, tapping her knuckles sharply on the car roof and getting no response. She's crazy out-of-her-mind about Benito with his confident air of command. The sleeves of his leather jacket are pushed up to display a green serpent tattoo on his left forearm. His buddies are hunched down and shivering in the bed of the pickup.

'Hector, Jesus, Ruben! Move it,' barks Benito. They grab their tools and pile out.

Hector slaps the flashlight against his thigh to keep the faltering batteries alive, while the others crank the jack handle, pop off a hubcap and wrench off the lug bolts. They unscrew the license plate and toss it in the bed of the truck.

While they're busy stripping the car, the girl rifles through the back of the wagon and finds a copy of that hot new book called *Peyton Place* with a Pickwick bookmark inside. A bottle of wine or carton of cigarettes would be better, but since the book is banned by the Pope, she at least wants to read the juicy parts.

'Stop messing around,' snaps Benito. 'See if he has a wallet.' She sets the book on top of the car and opens the driver's door. The gringo's body slumps against her. She gives a startled cry and stumbles backward. She looks at her bloody hand and wipes it on her jeans.

'Jesus, Mary and Joseph! The poor sucker's dead,' she says.

Jesus and Ruben grab the stolen hubcaps and pile back in the truck. Fanta picks up the book but Hector snatches it away, ripping out pages, crumpling them into a ball.

'What the hell are you doing?'

'My prints are all over the place,' says Hector. 'You want me to go to the gas chamber?' He squirts the paper with lighter fluid, sets it on fire and tosses it onto a blanket in the back of the car.

'Let's go, let's go!' says Benito, thumping his palm on the steering wheel.

As they speed into the night, the station wagon glows like an orange jack-o-lantern in their rear-view mirror, flames blossoming behind the windows.

In an abandoned house with broken windows and trash on the floor, they get blitzed on beer. When the others pass out, Fanta settles on a torn mattress. Benito flops on top of her. She can barely breathe beneath his weight. When he starts snoring she whacks him on the head and rolls him onto the floor, glaring angrily into the darkness.

★ ★ ★

At 3:30 a.m. after calling L.A.P.D., the sheriff's office, the highway patrol and the hospitals, Amanda puts on her slippers, tosses a robe over her nightgown and goes down the outer stairs to get her book from the car. Gavin's BMW is in its designated slot and her station wagon is gone. She stands riveted to the spot, confused. Gavin is in love with his BMW. He never takes the station wagon. It's one more thing about tonight that doesn't make any sense.

'Gavin?' she says, peering into the deep shadows of the carport. She touches the hood of his car. It's cold. It hasn't been driven since Gavin came home from the office around five. All night she's given a description of the wrong vehicle to the police, the hospitals, to everyone. As she contemplates her next move, Dack Traynor's Dodge pulls into the empty space beside the BMW. He gets out and slams the door. The noise is jolting in the stillness.

'Mrs. Chase, what are you doing out here?' He struts over and she takes a step back. He smells of alcohol and sweat and there's a lipstick smear on the neck of his T-shirt.

With no make-up and her hair blowing softly around her face, his every obsession kicks in with a warm rush. No matter how hard he tries . . . and he doesn't try very hard . . . he can't get his neighbor's pretty young wife out of his head.

'I'm just worried,' she says. 'Gavin should have been home hours ago.'

'I wouldn't worry about it. He probably had a flat or something.'

'He'd have found a way to call me.' The wind comes up and ripples the lacy hem of her nightgown. Dack takes a step

51

toward her. He touches her shoulder and she flinches.

'It's freezing out here. Let me see you to your door . . . Amanda.'

The intimate way he says her name reminds her how dark and isolated the carport is, how uncomfortably close he's standing. She turns and flies up the stairs, a shiver running up her spine. Once inside the apartment, she throws the deadbolt and presses her back against the door.

Dack laughs out loud. 'Another time then.'

* * *

Hallinan and Boatwright park at the overlook fifty yards beyond the Adler house. The hills are black, the moon spilling off the edge of the sky's inverted bowl. The pre-dawn chill has set in, and miles away at the eastern end of Griffith Park the nightlights from the observatory cast a ghostly glow.

In 1896 the park was deeded to the city by wealthy capitalist Griffith J. Griffith, making its five square miles the largest municipal park in the nation with its fifty miles of bridle trails, rugged terrain and thriving wildlife population.

The park is G. J. Griffith's most famous legacy, unless you count the two years he spent in San Quentin for shooting and partially blinding his wife while in a self-described state of alcoholic insanity. The park is beautiful and wild, beloved of photographers with its secret caves and scenic gulches. It's also an infamous body dump site.

There are two patrol cars parked at the overlook when they arrive. Down a jagged path that twists eastward through thick chaparral, a trio of flashlights bob through the darkness.

'Well, let's do it,' says Hallinan.

They walk to the wrought-iron gate of the pink house and climb the steps leading to the front door. Halfway to the entrance a second set of stairs angles off the main path and runs along the right side of the building to the back. Ornamental shrubs and herbs grow in large terracotta urns on the edges of the steps, and a ficus with a braided trunk grows in a planter box to the left of the front door.

Sergeant Paul Garner meets them in the foyer. He's a good-natured officer in his fifties. He's failed the lieutenant's exam three times, but he's a damn good meat-and-potatoes cop.

On the far side of the entry is a staircase leading down to the kitchen and dining area. Up a few steps to the right is the living room, occupied by a small assembly of exhausted people. A colorful clutter of wrapping paper, balloons and party hats are scattered around the room, champagne glasses and ashtrays on every surface. A staircase on the back wall of the living room leads to the next level.

'Strongbow is upstairs with Dr. Adler,' says Garner. 'Mrs. Adler was about to give a statement when the doctor injected her with a sedative. She's out like a light.'

'Interesting,' said Hallinan.

'That's what I thought. The fingerprint team is up in the child's room now.'

He and Tug enter the front room and Garner makes the necessary introductions. Dr. Adler's Aunt Sarah sits on the sofa beneath the arched windows, twisting a lace handkerchief. On the love seat, stage star Trudy Shawn has wilted against the shoulder of her agent, Todd Sinclair; and sitting alone by the fireplace is the Swedish au pair, Sigrid Nordgren, with her back turned to everyone.

'So far the search hasn't turned up anything we can run with,' says Garner. 'Might not hurt to call Elmer Wood and get his bloodhounds out here.'

'Good idea. Run with it,' says Hallinan. Garner heads downstairs to use the phone in the kitchen.

Sarah Adler is a retired French teacher living in the Fairfax District near Farmer's Market. Trudy Shawn resides at the Hollywood Studio Club while looking for a house to rent, and Todd Sinclair has a suite at the Hollywood Roosevelt Hotel.

Trudy and Todd canvased the hillside neighborhood, Trudy in high heels that raised painful blisters on her feet. Hallinan takes their statements, their contact information and lets them leave.

Trudy gives Tug a wink as she heads out the door. Hallinan sends him outside to look around while he interviews Sarah Adler in Helen's downstairs den. Sarah last remembers seeing Daisy going upstairs just before midnight after a brief appearance at the party. Sometime within the next hour she was gone.

'All of the bedrooms, plus Nathan's den, are on the third level,' she tells Hallinan. 'There's the front door leading to the outside, another off the downstairs dining room that opens onto the side patio, one to the front living room balcony, two leading to the back patio, one from the master bedroom and one from Daisy's room.'

'Who else went upstairs in the course of the evening?' says Hallinan.

'Anyone who wanted to. Mostly when the downstairs bathroom was occupied.'

'How many people were in the house tonight?'

'Maybe sixty when things were in full swing. The guest book would be helpful, but a photographer named Horst Kepler took off with it.'

'You mean he stole it?'

'Just pushed me aside and ran. Oh, how I'd like to wring that man's neck.

56

Calls himself Photographer To The Stars. That's Hollywood. Everyone has to be Something To The Stars. He launched Daisy's modeling career. A bunch of nonsense if you ask me.'

'Why would he want the guest book?' asks Hallinan.

'The signatures, I suppose. Lana Turner was here with Johnny Stompanato and a lot of big-shot movie people whose names I can't remember. Perhaps Kepler thinks he can sell it, or maybe he's just an aggravating putz.'

'That's all for now. If you think of anything else we can talk in the morning.'

Garner meets him back in the front room. 'Wood is in Bakersfield on another job, but he'll be here with the dogs by noon tomorrow if the traffic's not too heavy.'

'Good. Call Sunset Stable. They keep a list of volunteers. Have them organize a mounted patrol for the morning.'

Tug comes in from the outside with nothing remarkable to report. He offers to help Garner organize tomorrow's search.

'I'll take the Nordgren girl next,' says

Hallinan. 'She looks like someone sent her to Siberia. And Tug, tell Strongbow I want to see Dr. Adler as soon as he's through with him.'

4

Portrait in Ice

Sigrid Nordgren sits across the desk from Hallinan. She's striking in an outdoorsy way, tall and erect with a thick russet braid falling over one shoulder. She has a winter tan and ice-blue eyes. It's easy to imagine her scaling an alp with a 30-lb. pack riding like a feather on her back.

She wears tan slacks and a simple white blouse. Sitting in front of the fireplace with her head turned to the side, Hallinan hadn't noticed the red swelling on the left side of her face. She sits with her legs crossed, a sandal embellished with a tiger-eye medallion dangling casually from her big toe.

Hallinan takes out his notebook. 'I imagine this has been a difficult evening for you, Miss Nordgren.'

'Call me Sigrid. It will make things go faster.' He resists the urge to ask her if she has another pressing engagement.

'All right, Sigrid. How long have you been employed by the Adlers?'

'Six months.'

'And you live in?'

'I do.'

'In the capacity of babysitter?'

'That is correct.'

'How old are you, Sigrid?'

'Nineteen. I will be twenty in August.'

'Have you had previous experience caring for small children?'

'Not much. It's not a complicated job.'

'You mean it's not complicated until a child goes missing. Then it's not so simple anymore.' She does not respond. 'How would you describe Daisy Adler?'

'She is no trouble.'

Perhaps it's the cultural divide, but that seems an odd reply considering the number of things she might have said. She's cute. She's adorable. She likes storybooks. She's like a little sister to me.

'Would you care to elaborate?' He shifts in the chair, tapping his pen on the desktop.

'She is good-natured and obedient.'

Once again, the minimal response. He takes a few notes, adds a doodle or two.

'You are writing this down?' she asks.

'Does that bother you?'

'No. You may continue.'

That brings a slight smile to his face. 'Thank you. Do you enjoy working for the Adlers?'

'It is a job. It is good for learning English.'

'Yes, your English is very good. But what I mean is, do you find satisfaction in what you're doing? Do they pay you well? Is the atmosphere harmonious?'

'It is okay. I manage.'

'Do you think you could be a little more forthcoming, Sigrid? This isn't an episode of *Dragnet*. I need your impressions as well as the facts.' She nods. 'When did you last see Daisy?'

'I put her to bed at 9:00 p.m. She usually goes to bed a little earlier, but because of the party she got to stay up longer.'

'Did you check on her after that?'

'No. I didn't know she was gone until Mrs. Adler came looking for me.'

'Did you know that Daisy had gone downstairs around midnight?'

'Not until later. She seldom gets out of bed once I put her down.'

'Where were you between 11:00 p.m. and the time Mrs. Adler noticed that her daughter was not in her bed?'

A slight hesitation. 'I was down the hall from her room.'

'Not downstairs at the party.'

'Correct. It was a formal event. I was not invited.'

'Did you see anything suspicious, anyone loitering around her room?'

'No.'

'You said you were down the hall. Could you be more specific?'

'I was in the den.'

'Alone?'

She gives him a cool stare. 'No. Does it matter?'

'I don't know yet.'

'I was with Nathan, if you must know.'

'Nathan?' Not Mr. Adler or Dr. Adler? Or my boss. Just Nathan.

'He asked me to call him by his first name. Also, he calls me Sigrid.'

'And you call Mrs. Adler, Helen, I suppose.'

'I call her Mrs. Adler, of course.'

'Of course. Are you suggesting your relationship with Dr. Adler is more than that of employer/employee?'

'I wish to say no more on the subject.'

'You don't like her, do you? Mrs. Adler, I mean.'

'She is not very likable. You will see for yourself.'

'She probably thinks you have designs on her husband. How likable do you expect her to be?'

'What does that mean, designs?'

'That you envision a future with the doctor.'

She leans forward, her smile as cold as that immoveable object that sank the Titanic. 'He may be an old fool, Detective Hallinan, but I am not. In six months I go home and marry my boyfriend, Leif Jorgenson.'

'Wow! How would your young man feel about your recreational diversions?'

She shrugs. 'We don't read so much into it as Americans do.'

'Like Helen, you mean? Did she catch you two together?'

'She guessed.'

'And that's why he sedated her?'

'Between her anger with me and the dog tracks on the patio, she had become difficult. That's Helen, making a big deal over every small thing.'

Hallinan leans forward with renewed interest. 'What about the dog tracks?'

'She saw dog tracks on the patio behind her daughter's room and decided they were from a coyote. Her hysterics placed her center stage, exactly where she wanted to be.'

'Did you report this to the officers when they first arrived?'

'Why would I repeat such foolishness?'

'What do you think happened to Daisy Adler tonight, Miss Nordgren?'

'She is not a child who wanders off by herself. It is very upsetting. I'm through talking. I've told you everything I know.'

'You need to make yourself available in case I have more questions. And one more thing. I'll need to hold your passport until further notice.'

'My passport?'

'Yes, your passport.'

'It's in front of you. Mrs. Adler keeps it in the top desk drawer.'

He finds it on top a stack of envelopes. 'You may go,' he says.

'You understand I cannot stay here now.'

'I suppose not. We'll put you up elsewhere for the time being.'

There's a knock at the door and Officer Strongbow sticks his head in. 'Excuse me, sir. I'm through questioning Dr. Adler. Here are my notes. The fingerprint team has just left.' Hallinan skims over the notes and hands them back.

'Thank you, Sergeant. Please call Miss Williams at the Studio Club. Miss Nordgren needs a place to stay short term. She can bill the department. Is that agreeable, Miss Nordgren?'

'I'll just collect a few things.'

'Get her checked in, Lance, then go home and get some shut-eye. I'd like you back here at eight to man the phones in case a ransom call comes in. Did Dr. Adler mention anything about dogs or coyotes when you spoke with him?'

'Not a word. Is it important?'

'It could be.'

Sergeant Garner enters the room as Strongbow leaves.

'Paul, I'd like a tracer put on this line. Have an officer man the phones until Strongbow takes over in the morning.'

'Yes sir.' Garner hands him a slip of paper. 'That's the business address of Horst Kepler. Find out anything helpful from Miss Nordgren?'

'While the party was going on downstairs, she and Adler were upstairs having a little party of their own.'

'Now there's an image for you.'

★ ★ ★

Hallinan stands with Nathan Adler outside his daughter's room in the upstairs hall. He's of average height and weight, with a mid-life paunch and a forgettable man-in-the-crowd face. The contrast between Adler's pale flab and Sigrid's healthy scaffolding is an image Hallinan tries not to dwell on.

'When is Sigrid coming up?' says Adler, patting his empty breast pocket for cigarettes. 'I'd really like her with me.'

Hallinan doesn't respond. He taps a Chesterfield from his pack, hands it to Adler and lights it with his Ronson.

'Helen would kill me if she saw me smoking upstairs,' he says. 'The smell gets in the curtains.'

'Dr. Adler, I understand two doors on this level open to the outside?'

'What? Oh yes, the double doors in the master bedroom and a single in Daisy's room. Why don't you look around while I work on my smoke?'

Hallinan enters the child's room. There's fingerprint powder on the woodwork, no obvious disarray in the room, no signs of struggle.

'Do you keep the doors and windows locked?'

'I've never thought about it,' says Adler from the doorway. 'There's no crime to speak of in this area. Helen may have locked Daisy's door earlier in the evening, but it was unlocked when she discovered her empty bed.'

'You might consider locking the house at night. There was no crime in Charles Lindbergh's neighborhood, until his child was kidnapped and murdered.'

'You're not suggesting foul play? The worst thing that ever happened on Fairbanks was a man holding Mrs. Alpert's poodle for ransom.'

'I'm simply saying that living in an upscale neighborhood can create a false sense of security.'

Hallinan opens the French door and steps onto the patio. The area has already been cordoned off. The flagstones run the width of the house and abut the hillside at the back of the property. The wind is up, an owl hoots from a nearby tree and a nocturnal animal skitters unseen through the chaparral.

Hallinan walks the length of the patio, checks the windows at the back of the house and finds them firmly secured. After reviewing Strongbow's notes and looking around, he believes that whatever happened tonight most likely happened here.

Adler rubs out his cigarette on the sole

of his shoe and joins Hallinan. He's about to flick the butt on the patio when Hallinan stops him. 'Don't contaminate the scene, sir.' Adler transfers the butt to the cuff of his trousers. 'Do you know what time this door was locked?'

'Helen said around eight.'

'It would be helpful if I could speak with her.'

'She requested sedation. She was too distraught to be questioned.' It's a lie, but Hallinan lets it pass for the moment.

'Would Daisy go out this door by herself?'

'After dark? Probably not.'

'Is this where Mrs. Adler saw the coyote tracks?'

After a telling moment of silence, Adler says, 'What tracks?'

'I think you know what tracks, sir.'

'Who told you that? They were d-dog tracks. It was n-nothing.'

'The tracks of a medium-sized dog and a coyote would be indistinguishable from one another, unless you know something about canines that I don't,' says Hallinan.

Adler runs a hand over his thinning

hair. The wind streams through the chaparral and scrub oak. Among the dead leaves at his feet Hallinan sees a flutter of green in the glow from the bug light. He bends over and picks up a crisp ten-dollar bill by a corner.

'Wonder how that got here?' says Adler.

Hallinan takes a glassine envelope from his pocket and puts the bill inside. Back in the room he asks Adler what he knows about Kepler.

'He's very popular from all I've heard. In fact, I'll show you a sample of his work.' They step inside and he takes a 5 by 7 framed photo from a shelf above his daughter's bed. She stands smiling in a ruffled pink dress beside a small pony in a carnival setting. She's an exceptionally beautiful child.

'May I borrow this?'

The doctor removes the photo from its frame and Hallinan places it carefully between the pages of his notebook. They step into the hall. 'What else do you know about Kepler?'

'I never met the man before tonight, but he spent the entire evening annoying my guests with his camera.'

'Do you know he stole the guest book?'

'You must be kidding. You can't trust anyone these days.' Hallinan finds the comment ironic coming from a man who's sleeping with the babysitter under his wife's nose. 'I can't imagine him doing anything unless there's money in it.'

'Do you keep a list of invited guests?'

'Helen would have one in her files.'

'Can you think of anyone who's taken an unhealthy interest in your daughter?'

'Of course not! What kind of a question is that?'

'Are you involved in a lawsuit or neighborhood dispute?'

'No.'

'How about a disagreement over money or an unfriendly rivalry, personal or professional? Any pending lawsuits?'

'None of the above.'

'How about a botched facelift?'

'You're a real asshole, you know that, Hallinan?'

Hallinan smiles. 'Can you think of anyone who might want to get at you or your wife by harming your daughter?'

'Helen and I don't make enemies.'

'Would you say your marriage is a happy one?' A sheen of sweat appears on Adler's forehead. The polygraph in Hallinan's head is set on record.

Adler gives Hallinan a befuddled look. 'I don't know how this line of questioning is helpful in finding my daughter.'

'You didn't answer the question.'

'What question?'

'About your marriage. Is it harmonious?'

After several beats, Adler says, 'You've been talking to Sigrid.'

'Let's say I know how you celebrated your birthday.'

Adler's face flushes. 'How dare you question my employee outside of my presence?'

Hallinan can't help smiling. 'You mean before you had a chance to get your stories straight? Why did you sedate Mrs. Adler? Sergeant Strongbow said she was about to give a voluntary statement.'

'What do you think?'

'I forgot my crystal ball. Why don't you tell me?'

'I didn't want her babbling. She'll do

whatever it takes to implicate Sigrid in Daisy's disappearance.'

'Why would she do that, Dr. Adler?'

'She's furious with Sigrid. She put Teddy's cat food and water bowl outdoors. Helen says leaving food out attracts wild-life. Leave it to Helen to leap to dramatic conclusions — mountain lions . . . coyotes . . . the Golem of Prague! She struck Sigrid in front of our guests and called her an insulting name. I sedated Helen to pre-vent further embarrassment.'

'Embarrassment to you, you mean. You didn't want her talking about Sigrid. You wanted to make sure she didn't mention the argument or the animal tracks. Now, I'd like to see the cat's bowls and the tracks.'

'I brought the bowls inside and cleaned up the mess. There was no blood. I think that proves my point.'

'Not necessarily. A coyote would do a snatch and run, drag his prey to a place where he felt safe before settling in with it.'

'We would have heard something. There would have been screams.'

'I agree, but with a noisy party going on, I'm not sure anyone would have heard her. Listen, Doctor, you tamper with any more evidence and you will have more trouble than you can talk your way out of. You have no idea the value of the evidence you may have destroyed.'

'I get it. Are we almost through here?'

'You don't seem to be all that broken up about your daughter's disappearance. Why is that?'

Adler flexes the muscles in his jaw. He pats his pocket but this time Hallinan lets him sweat. 'Because Helen is probably behind this charade. She has Daisy stashed somewhere all safe and sound.'

'If you have proof to back that up, I'd certainly like to see it.'

'She thinks if she creates a three-ring circus I won't . . . '

'You won't what?'

'Walk out on her.'

Sigrid was right. He is an old fool. 'You can't be thinking of leaving your wife for the babysitter.'

'Why not? I only have so many good years left. My marriage has been stagnant for years. This could be my last chance to grab the gold ring.'

Oh boy, it sounds like Adler is about to jump off the deep end. Too bad there's no water in the pool.

'I want to see Mrs. Adler now,' says Hallinan.

'I told you, she's . . . '

'Now, Dr. Adler, or I will charge you with obstructing an officer in the performance of his duty.'

Adler stomps across the hall to the master bedroom. He stands at the door with his arms crossed over his chest as Hallinan brushes by him. Mrs. Adler lies beneath a flowered quilt. The pale rose carpet in her room is soft and deep and a lamp burns dimly on the nightstand.

Hallinan bends over and touches her hand. It's fragile and webbed with delicate blue veins. Her breathing is shallow and even, her pulse rate slow but within normal parameters. Her golden gown is in a pile on the floor.

'Does your wife have a personal physician?'

'Yes, Dr. Sheldon Rappaport in Beverly

Hills, if you must know.'

'I want him here within the hour. You stay away from this woman with your needles and pills. You're not to treat her for as much as a common cold or I'll have you thrown behind bars. Is that understood?'

Adler fumes with barely restrained anger, a big shot not used to taking orders from anyone, especially a lowly flatfoot.

'Did you hear me?' says Hallinan, in the kind of quiet voice that carries a hint of menace.

'Yes.'

Hallinan walks past him, then turns back. 'Hang up your wife's dress, Dr. Adler. Have some respect for the mother of your child.'

★ ★ ★

When Hallinan leaves the pink house, the eastern sky is turning grey and Tug is briefing the officers in charge of organizing the search party. Horse trailers are parked at the overlook, riders saddling up, opening bags of donuts and drinking coffee from paper cups. There's a stiff breeze coming down from the north and a few wisps of dark cloud on the horizon. A large tiger-striped tomcat is sleeping in a bed of spearmint next to the garage. He bends down and runs his hand over the battle-scarred head. 'So, you're Teddy,' he says. 'You've caused a lot of trouble, you know.'

The cat looks up with big golden eyes, then curls into a comfortable ball and buries his nose in the tip of his tail. Hallinan signals to Tug and they compare notes on the investigation. He shows Tug the bill he found on the back patio as they cruise down the hill.

'Maybe it was dropped by the abductor,' says Tug.

'Possibly. If there is an abductor.'

'Look — what's that in the corner?'

Hallinan squints at the ten-dollar bill. 'Green ink. Looks like a horseshoe.'

'Sure does.'

Confetti and crêpe-paper streamers blow through the deserted intersections. Hallinan looks at the address Garner gave him. 'Drive down LaBrea,' says Hallinan.

'Let's have a look at Kepler's studio.'

They swing a right on Hollywood Blvd, and take a left on LaBrea a few blocks later. The studio is a high-rent art deco half a block off the main drag. They pull to the curb and Hallinan jogs up to the door. Back in the car he says, 'It's closed Dec. 20th through January 1st. This is one guy we need to talk to.'

'I'll run a background check and see if any skeletons jump out of the closet.' He pops a breath mint in his mouth. 'What did the nanny have to say?'

'She and Adler were having a private celebration while the guests rang in the New Year. He thinks they're going to ride off into the sunset like Roy Rogers and Dale Evans, but she told me she's returning to Sweden to marry her fiancé.'

'I'd call that a major breakdown in communications,' says Tug, snorting a laugh.

'Adler would like us to believe that his wife has Daisy hidden away, but that seems a bit far-fetched.'

'I think so too, but stranger things have happened.'

'That brings us to the coyote theory,' says Hallinan. 'Know anything about coyotes?'

'They're smart and opportunistic and they're all over these hills. They've killed several pets in the area and I don't think they'd make a distinction between a forty-pound dog and a forty-pound child.'

'I think it's something we have to take seriously.'

'Did you hear that Lana Turner was at the party with Johnny Stompanato?' says Tug.

'Sarah Adler mentioned it.'

'They're tight with the Adlers. Lana's probably had a nip-and-tuck done by the illustrious doctor.'

'There's a rumor Stompanato is trying to hit Turner up for a fifty-thousand-dollar loan so he can produce a movie and star in it. They've been having some nasty brawls. You know why Turner's with him, don't you?' says Hallinan.

Tug gives him a sidelong glance. 'He's a blue-ribbon stud, but she doesn't strike me as a woman who leaves her brain on the pillow. I hear they've had some nasty brawls and her teenage daughter is caught in the middle. At least Stompanato keeps a lower profile than that clown he works for.'

'Don't be fooled by Cohen's third-grade education,' says Hallinan. 'You don't have to know advanced math when you measure your money by the inch. Mickey was tough enough, at five feet three inches, to take over the rackets when they cancelled Siegel's ticket. Chief Parker would love to nail him, but it's like nailing Jello to the wall. I have a sneaking admiration for the guy.'

'Parker is just mad because Cohen's crew took over all the operations that used to be controlled by the vice cops,' says Tug. They drive for a couple blocks in silence. 'What if Turner and Stompanato signed the guest book? That could be the motive for Kepler making off with it.'

'You mean blackmail? I don't know, Tug. Their secret ain't much of a secret.'

'True, but one of the slander sheets might try to implicate him in Daisy Adler's disappearance. It doesn't have to be true to sell papers. Look what rumors did to Fatty Arbuckle. The studios dropped him like a hot potato and he died a pauper.'

Tug pulls off Washington Blvd., then onto Sandalwood Street a couple blocks later. 'Well, here we are.'

'Let's grab some shut-eye,' says Hallinan. 'I want to be back up there when the dogs arrive.'

'Great. That gives us a full three hours.'

5

The Scent of Danger

It's a raucous New Year's Eve at Club Velvet. By the time the curtain falls, the stage is littered with broken bottles and trash. Crystal has been grabbed, groped and humiliated. Abdominal pain makes it impossible to concentrate on dancing.

Back in her dressing room she looks in the mirror. She can't believe how much weight she's lost in so short a period of time. She wraps herself in a chenille robe and drops her tips in her jewelry box. She's always had luxurious hair. Now she's wears a wig to cover the bald spots.

Cesar said Crystal could have New Year's Eve off, but he'd grown suspicious and changed his mind. She wonders how long Gavin had waited for her before he realized she wasn't coming. It would have been their last time together anyway. She could feel his ardor cooling, his anxiety peaking. It's always the wife who wins in the end. At least for a while she could pretend.

The dressing room door bursts open and Cesar marches in from the cold. His face is hard and unreadable and there's a pungent metallic odor on his clothes. He takes a gun out of his pocket, opens the floor safe and locks it inside.

'What are you doing with the gun?' she asks, feeling a little sick to her stomach.

'Protecting my financial interests.'

She's afraid to ask what he means because she already knows. Hearing the words would be more than she can handle. She'd rather go on pretending.

'I bumped into Mildred Grassley at the fights the other night,' says Cesar.

'Who?'

'The nurse. She tells me she hasn't seen you since that first time two years ago.'

'She's lying. The old butcher took the money the moment I walked through the door. Her hand is a bear trap.'

'How much you make in tips tonight?'

'I don't know. The money's in the jewelry box.'

He dumped the contents on the vanity and scoops the money into his pocket. 'There's maybe twenty here. Now you owe me one eighty.'

'The old bat has your money. Why don't you squeeze it out of her?'

'If you couldn't stand up to her, it's on you.'

There was no sense arguing. 'Listen Cesar, we have to talk. The doctor who examined me says I need to follow up. You can see how sick I am. He says I need surgery.'

'Just stick to your job. A stripper with a purple scar across her belly isn't worth much in this world . . . '

★　★　★

Hallinan limps up the porch steps, but instead of Beezer's little wags and yips, he's greeted by a creaking floorboard and the sound of wind in the chimney. He closes the flue. As he turns up the thermostat he notices the empty space beneath the window where his mother's piano had been. In its place is a scratch in the hardwood floor.

He spins a litany of weary expletives. What did Dorothy do, come with George Atlas and a moving van? On the dining room table is a manila envelope with an attorney's name in the upper left hand corner.

'Welcome home, Rusty,' he says.

He smokes aggressively while he makes a pot of coffee, warms up a couple of cans of chili con carne and half a leftover pizza. He settles down at the dining-room table with the ominous-looking envelope beside his cup.

After he's eaten he has a third cup of coffee, lights another cigarette and finally works up the courage to open the envelope. There are forms and more forms, each numbered line in lawyerly capital letters.

Seems Dorothy has one small obstacle in obtaining a divorce. No legitimate grounds. Hallinan has never committed adultery and doesn't have a 'loathsome disease'. He's neither mentally incompetent nor physically abusive. He's not criminally insane or confined to a penal institution. Therefore, suggests Haverson Rumford, Esquire, Hallinan should be a good sport and go along with Dorothy's accusation of infidelity. It would expedite the process and avoid the expense of lengthy courtroom wrangling.

He returns the forms to the envelope, rinses his dishes and goes upstairs to bed. He's barely drifted off when he wakes to the rumble of thunder. The room is dark, a wall of rain battering the windowpane. He jumps out of bed, one thought tumbling over the next: the search . . . the horses . . . the tracking dogs.

Within five minutes he's showered, dressed and downstairs. As he pours cereal in a bowl, Dorothy comes through the door in a glossy red raincoat. She is fashion-model thin with a wasp waist and coltish legs. She shakes out her umbrella on the hardwood floor and he moves his bowl aside.

'If you'd been here earlier I wouldn't have had to make a second trip,' she says.

'Stanek pulled me off R and R. A child's gone missing and I'm lead detective on the case.'

'There's no one gets it done like the great Rusty Hallinan.'

'Why don't you come home, Dorothy? There's nothing wrong that we can't work out.'

'I've come for the papers.'

He hands her the envelope and watches her remove the documents.

'I hope you signed on the proper lines,' she says.

'I won't put my name to a pack of lies for the sake of expedience.' She glares at him and throws the envelope back on the table. 'Why did you take the piano, Dorothy? You don't even play. First you take my dog, then you take my piano.'

'Because you don't get it yet,' she says.

'What's to get?'

'I want a divorce and I don't want it dragged out.'

Hallinan extends his hand. 'Give me my house keys.'

'When you sign the papers.'

It would have been easy to wrestle them from her hand. Instead he walks to the door and opens it.

'Goodbye, Dorothy.'

After she's gone, Hallinan switches the front and back door lock sets, each requiring a different key. She might figure it out, but it's the best he can do on short notice. As he returns the screwdriver to the toolbox, the phone rings. It's Captain Stanek.

'Bad news, Rusty. The dogs can't work in this weather and the trails are too slippery for the horses, but we still have a sizable party searching on foot.' Stanek clears his throat. 'I have another reason for calling. A man at the Castleton Apartments has gone missing. His name is Gavin Chase, a successful young architect.'

'When and where was he last seen?'

'At home. Nine-thirty or ten last night.'

'That's not missing, Captain. That's being late for dinner.'

Stanek laughs. 'I know his wife. She was in my son's senior class. She's been calling the desk every five minutes.' Hallinan scribbles down the apartment number. 'Go see what she has to say. Her name is Amanda Chase.'

* * *

Hallinan pulls into the lot at the Castleton Apartments. The sky is black, rain clattering like buckshot on the roof of the Buick. It's a well-maintained complex tucked into a leafy knoll above Franklin Avenue.

Hallinan's knee aches from the damp as he walks past a dripping hedge of juniper and up a flight of concrete stairs to the second level. He knocks on door 212. The door opens and a pretty young woman in jeans, blue T-shirt and bare feet stands in the doorway. She's about five two or three with long-lashed blue-green eyes, no make-up and golden-brown hair falling in a casual tangle. She looks like she's been up all night.

'Mrs. Chase?'

'Yes.'

'I'm Lieutenant Hallinan. Captain Stanek asked me to come by. I understand you're concerned about your husband.'

'Yes, please come in,' she says, stepping back from the door. 'Let me take your coat. I'm surprised the captain remembers me. It's been six years since high school.'

Hallinan can't imagine anyone forgetting her, even if they'd met her once. As she helps him shrug out of his coat, her hair brushes against his shoulder. It's soft and lavender-scented and sends a little shiver up his arm.

'Please, won't you sit?' she says, hanging his coat on the hall tree. She points to a white leather sofa facing a television set. He squeezes behind an antique trunk that serves as a coffee table and sinks deep into the cushion. Those extra pounds. They've got to go.

'I just made coffee. Let me pour you a cup.'

'That would be nice, thank you. Black, no sugar is fine,' he calls after her.

He looks around the room. There's an overflowing bookcase, a desk, a set of antique Chinese chairs, a Kandinsky print on the wall above a drafting table, three examples of pre-Columbian pottery, and a giant fern in a hanging pot.

She returns with two cups and settles next to him, her feet tucked beneath her. 'I'm worried sick about my husband,' she says. 'I can't stop looking out the window.

I've been running through every possible scenario and nothing makes sense. I can generally set my watch by Gavin, but last night he left around ten to run an errand and never returned.'

'Did he say where he was going?'

'No, only that he wouldn't be long.'

'Do you have an idea where he might have gone?'

'I assumed to pick up a hostess gift, maybe a bottle of champagne. We were expected at a friend's New Year's party.'

'Has he disappeared like this before?'

'Never.'

'Did you have a disagreement last night?'

'No. We were both in a good mood.'

'Does he drink to excess?'

'No. He'll have a drink, maybe two, but I've never seen him drunk. We're in the process of purchasing a house. Gavin is very excited about overseeing the restoration.' She takes a thoughtful sip from her cup. 'There is something about last night, however . . . something that I can't explain.'

'What's that, Mrs. Chase?'

'Gavin drives a BMW. He's crazy about that car. The only time he's taken my station wagon was when his went in for an oil change. When I went down to the carport several hours after midnight, I found his car here and mine gone. It doesn't make any sense. All evening I'd given the police a description of the wrong car.'

'Tell me about the car he was driving.'

She sets her cup on the trunk and walks to the desk. 'I have paperwork from the dealership right here.'

'I imagine you've called around.'

'Of course. I've called everyone. I've called Sergeant Dunnigan until he won't talk to me anymore,' she says, returning with the papers on a white 1954 Chevy station wagon. Hallinan writes down the license and vin number.

'Mrs. Chase . . . '

'Just Amanda. Mrs. Chase is Gavin's mother.'

'Then I'm Rusty,' he says. 'My mother wanted an Irish setter puppy for Christmas, but she got me instead.'

She tilts her head to the side. 'Is that really true?'

'Scout's honor.'

'I'm glad the captain didn't send someone who thinks I'm a nutcase. First I give Sergeant Dunnigan the description of a black BMW, then tell him it's a white station wagon. What else could he think?' Amanda glances at the TV. 'Do you mind? I'd like to know how long this rain is going to last. I worry more when the weather is bad.'

'Go ahead,' he says, equally curious to know if the Daisy Adler disappearance has leaked to the media. She crosses the room and switches it on. She turns up the volume. A reporter in a rain slicker is speaking from what appears to be the scene of an auto accident. Behind him are three police cars with lights flashing, a fire truck and a tow truck. As Hallinan leans forward an ambulance appears on the scene.

'It looks like a bad one,' says Amanda.

'At three a.m. this morning,' says the reporter, 'the police were alerted to a car fire in lower Boyle Heights. The partially burned body of a male adult was discovered behind the wheel. Official cause of death is pending, but onlookers say the driver has what appears to be a bullet wound to the side of his head. Let's move in for a closer look,' he says, pressing through the crowd of onlookers. He steps aside to give the cameraman a better shot of the accident site. The car is a white station wagon, the windows blackened by smoke, the license plate missing.

'That car is similar . . . ' says Amanda, 'but it couldn't possibly . . . I'm afraid I'm not feeling very . . . ' As she looks pleadingly at Hallinan, the light goes out in her eyes. He's already on his feet, moving toward her. Her face is white; her knees give way. He catches her as she collapses and he carefully eases her to the floor, her hair fanning out on the carpet. He rubs her hands in both of his. They're cold and limp.

'Amanda! Amanda! Jesus Christ!'

Hallinan jumps up, grabs the phone on the desk and calls for an ambulance. By the time it arrives, Amanda is regaining consciousness and doubled up in pain. He walks beside the stretcher as the attendants load her into the ambulance.

94

'What's happening?' asks Hallinan. 'What's wrong with her?'

'I believe your wife is having a miscarriage, Mr. Chase.'

Hallinan doesn't bother correcting him. He watches the ambulance pull away and runs back up the stairs to the apartment. He calls Stanek, tells him what's happened and gives him the vitals on the station wagon.

'I'll call Hollenbeck Division and see what I can find out,' says Stanek. 'Keep me posted on her condition. Don't drop the ball on this.'

Amanda's purse is on the kitchen counter. Inside are keys to the apartment, the BMW and the station wagon. He puts them in his pocket, pulls on his raincoat, steps onto the walkway and locks the door behind him.

A man comes out of 214 posturing like a delinquent on the cover of a paperback novel: black bomber jacket, tight jeans, cigarette dangling from his mouth.

'I thought I heard a siren.'

'Me too,' says Hallinan. 'Must have gone up the hill.'

'If you're here to see the lovely Miss Amanda, she's one of those buttoned-up types. She's married, you know, although what she sees in him is beyond me.'

What an odd specimen. 'Are you rehearsing a script?' asks Hallinan.

'I don't know. Do you think I'll get the part?'

This is getting weirder and weirder.

'I'm Officer Hallinan with L.A.P.D. And you are?'

That seems to throw him off his game for a second. 'For all I know you're the Fuller Brush Man,' he says, a little of the cockiness gone now.

'Does the Fuller Brush man have one of these?' says Hallinan, flipping his shield. 'What did you say your name is again?'

'I think I hear my mother calling,' he says, flicking his cigarette butt in the rain and vanishing inside 214. Hallinan smiles to himself. That was certainly an odd encounter.

Hallinan walks to the carport and uses Amanda's extra key to get inside the BMW. The car smells expensive, like new Italian leather shoes. He turns the engine over and it purrs like a cat. The tank is full, the headlights and windshield wipers operable. So why did Chase take his wife's car, and what is he doing in the barrios of Boyle Heights when he was expected at a Hollywood party?

He locks the vehicle and walks to the manager's office. Behind the counter is an elderly gentleman in a dress shirt and bow tie. Hallinan knows him from past calls to the Castleton.

'What's going on, Hallinan?' says Alvin Hornsby. 'I saw the ambulance.'

'Someone had a fainting spell. What's the name of the guy in 214?'

'Dack Traynor. He's seen *The Wild One* too many times.'

'Single?'

'No, he's got a wife who works at the bank, but he doesn't act like any married man I ever knew.'

'Cause any problems?'

'He's a peeper. If Mr. Chase catches him at the bedroom window again, Dack won't live long enough to collect his next unemployment check. I'm writing up his eviction notice as we speak.'

6

Dark Secrets

On his way to Fairbanks Drive, Hallinan runs off a stack of missing-person flyers with a blow-up of the pony photo.

'Everyone in the household has been fingerprinted,' says Tug when Hallinan arrives on the scene. 'Any unidentified prints in the nursery will have to be run through the system.'

'They'll need Sigrid's to eliminate her from the mix.'

'They're on their way to the Studio Club now. I've talked with the aunt again, but she's told us everything she knows. Dr. Rappaport has come and gone. He said Adler gave his wife enough medication to knock out a herd of elephants. Adler hid in his den until Rappaport left, then drove off in his Mustang. He's been all over me about where we've stashed Sigrid. I figure she knows how to reach him if she wants to.'

'And Mrs. Adler?'

'She's in her room waiting for you.'

'Any calls?'

'Not from kidnappers.'

'As soon as the storm blows over we'll get the dogs and horses back on the job. Unless Daisy is recovered, or we get a ransom call by this evening, we'll get ready for a bombard from the media.'

Hallinan goes up the stairs. The bedroom door is open and Mrs. Adler waves him in.

'So you're Hallinan. Auburn hair. Blue eyes. They've sent me a cop straight from central casting.'

'This is Hollywood, Mrs. Adler.' Her eyes are red-rimmed from crying, but he sees the hint of a smile. She sits near the window looking out at the panorama of rain-swept hills. She wears jade-green lounging pajamas, à la Lauren Bacall, her hair pulled back in a chignon and run through with a carved ivory chopstick. She motions to the chair nearest her and Hallinan squeezes his bulk between the arm rests.

'I hear you're the one responsible for getting Rappaport over here.'

'Yes, ma'am.'

'That's good. Nathan's already given me the treatment,' she says with a wry glance. 'Too bad the weather is working against us today.'

'That doesn't mean the searchers are any less enthusiastic. We still have officers out there on foot.'

'If Daisy is in the hills, do you think she'd have survived the night?'

'Yes, ma'am, I do. Children are amazingly resilient. I've heard of newborn babies being pulled alive from collapsed buildings after a week without food or water.'

'Is it possible she's been abducted?'

'I don't know. Right now we're investigating every possibility.'

'And my coyote theory?'

'I've given it some thought. If his objective was to make off with Daisy, I think the cat food would have been left in the bowl.'

'That does make sense.' Her eyes drift back to the rain-swept hills rolling toward the eastern horizon. 'Are you a religious man?'

Hallinan considers the question. 'That depends on who you ask. I sometimes drink too much. I always eat too much, and I haven't been to confession in two years. On the other hand, I'm not on the take and I don't cheat on my wife, which is irrelevant, because she's leaving me for a younger man.'

She reaches over and pats his hand. 'You're okay, Lieutenant.' Her skin is waxen, almost translucent, and she has half-moon shadows beneath her eyes. 'Oh, how I hate this waiting game. I feel so helpless.'

'Have you eaten anything today, Mrs. Adler?'

'Maybe later. Sarah won't let me starve.' She gives a weary sigh. 'I regret slapping Sigrid. She's just a foolish teenager.'

'Maybe she needed a little slapping.'

They share a smile. 'Maybe she did. I was raised in this house, you know. When I married Nathan he was a young intern with one threadbare suit and a pair of worn-out shoes. Believe me, Lieutenant, being married to a doctor is no walk in the park. They're never home when you need them. Their patients think they're gods and they come to believe it. Somewhere along the way, I've become as dispensable as high-button shoes.'

'If your husband is smart he'll come to his senses.'

'Nathan?' She gives him an incredulous look. 'Don't bet on it, Lieutenant.'

She opens a drawer in the small table that separates their chairs. 'Here's the guest list. Some of the guests brought friends. Others didn't show, and not everyone signed the guest book, so I'm not sure how helpful this is going to be.'

Hallinan scans the list and folds it into his notebook. 'Thank you. It gives us a place to start. What can you tell me about Horst Kepler?'

'He never goes anywhere without his camera. Always has his ear to the ground and his eye to the keyhole, hoping for the money shot . . . a plane falling out of the sky . . . a politician in bed with an eighth-grader . . . a school bus dangling from an overpass. Inviting him was a serious lapse of judgment on my part.'

'I understand you locked Daisy's bedroom door in the early evening.'

'As well as the one off our bedroom. Ours was still locked when I checked later. There's a small catch at the top of Daisy's door frame. She can't reach it even if she stands on a chair. Sigrid unlocked it when she put out the cat food. I'm sure you've heard the whole story.' Wind gusts down the hill behind the house, sending a solid sheet of rain and dead leaves against the window. 'Do you think a reward might help?'

'We can talk about it if Daisy isn't back in a day or two. What we don't need right now is a litany of false confessions and fortune-hunters.'

'Yes, I see your point.'

'I'm going to look around outside, see if I missed anything in the dark.' He rises from his chair. 'One more thing,' he says, pulling out the glassine envelope. 'Would you look at this bill and tell me if it means anything to you?' She turns it over and examines both sides through the plastic.

'That's the ten Johnny Stompanato gave

Daisy last night. He draws a horseshoe on his money; says it brings him luck at the track. Where did you find it?'

'On the patio behind her room. We don't know what it means yet, if anything.'

'Oh, I think we do, Lieutenant,' she says. 'It means Daisy was on the patio after midnight.'

Hallinan passes under the yellow tape and climbs the rain-slick path behind the patio. From the top of the hill he scans the storm-whipped vista of hills. They seem to roll on forever. He sees something in the leaf litter at his feet and picks up a child's ponytail elastic decorated with blue plastic balls. Any viable footprints would have been washed away during the night. When he comes back down the hill, Mrs. Adler is standing on the patio beneath the dripping eaves. He shows her the found object.

'I wish it was relevant, Lieutenant. Daisy lost it when she was playing outdoors last summer.'

'It means that she was able to climb the hill six months ago. Whether she could climb it in the dark, I don't know. I want you to go inside. We can't have Daisy coming home to a sick mother.'

Hallinan continues his circuit of the property, finding nothing else of interest. When he returns to the house, the phone is ringing. Strongbow looks up as Hallinan and Tug come into the den. 'It's for you, Rusty,' he says. 'It's Miss Shawn.'

He takes the receiver. 'Hallinan here.' Tug listens, but most of the conversation comes from the other end. After a minute or two, Hallinan hangs up. 'Come on, Tug, we're going to the Studio Club. Miss Shawn has some information for us.'

*   *   *

The Hollywood Studio Club is a small Italian Renaissance hotel on Lodi, off Sunset and Vine. It was designed in the 1920s by Julia Morgan of San Simeon fame as a safe harbor for aspiring young actresses. It was from here that Marilyn Monroe and Kim Novak launched their careers.

Hallinan and Boatwright sign in at the desk and the receptionist buzzes Trudy's room. Moments later she appears in the company of a stunning Chinese girl with dark waist-long hair. Trudy wears a yellow wool dress with an energetic red scarf; her friend, an Oriental sheath of ruby brocade. Trudy introduces the officers to her roommate, Linda Kwan.

'Let's go to the music room where it's private,' says Trudy. 'I saw Sigrid at breakfast this morning. She wasn't exactly thrilled when the fingerprint guys showed up. A few of the girls offered to show her around, but she wasn't in a sociable mood.'

They follow the ladies down the corridor to a small room off the central courtyard. Beyond the window rain splashes on the stones, water dripping from giant ferns along the walkway. It's an intimate space dominated by a piano, a violin stand and a few upholstered chairs.

'Linda's an actress and model,' says Trudy when everyone is seated. 'I was telling her about Daisy Adler and the party on Fairbanks. When I mentioned Horst Kepler, she said she had a disturbing encounter with him last summer. Go ahead, Linda, tell them what you told me.'

'Last spring I did a layout for *Playboy*,' says Linda in a quiet, rather shy voice. 'When Horst saw the spread he called me. He said he was shooting an art film outside Chatsworth and would I like to see the set and read for a part. I thought it might be something to add to my list of credits, so we drove out the following Saturday.

'The area is remote, full of gullies and big boulders. Kepler pulled off the main road onto a dirt one-lane by a bar called Bud's Suds and drove about five more miles into the hills. I didn't expect to end up so far off the beaten path. I was feeling uncomfortable about being in so isolated a place without having told anyone where I was going. I could smell his nervous sweat and I started thinking about the Black Dahlia case and how she probably wasn't afraid until it was too late.

'Horst finally pulled up a steep driveway and parked in front of a weather-beaten building at an abandoned mine site. We went inside. It was storage for old mining equipment. He opened a second door. There were cameras and lights circling a movie set with a red velvet backdrop and a big heart-shaped bed in the center. I began to tremble.

'I said, 'I want to go home. I've changed my mind.' He grabbed my wrist and I started to cry. Horst was furious. He dragged me out of the building, shoved me in the van and drove back the way we'd come. He wouldn't stop yelling at me; said I'd wasted his time and I should pay for his gas. Can you believe it? I should pay for his gas? When he slowed at the intersection, I jumped out and twisted my ankle. I hobbled into Bud's Suds as Kepler sped away. I've never been so scared in my life.'

'How did you get back to town?' asks Hallinan.

'On the back of a Harley-Davidson. Normally, I wouldn't go off with a guy named Spike with a Born To Lose tattoo on his arm, but I was so relieved to get away from Kepler, I thought he looked like an angel. And I can't say Spike wasn't a perfect gentleman. When he dropped me off he said I should call him if I wanted Kepler whacked.'

'Wow!' says Trudy. 'He's a keeper. Can I have his number?'

Linda smiles and Tug laughs out loud. Linda reaches in her pocket and gives Hallinan Kepler's business card. 'I drew a map on the other side. It's the location of the abandoned mine. He's out there a great deal of the time.'

He tucks the card into his wallet. 'Why do you think Kepler wanted the Adlers' guest book?'

'He said something odd the day I met him. I told him I was impressed by all the famous people he knew. He said, 'Linda, it's not who you know, it's what you know about who you know.''

'You took that to mean what?'

'He was talking about blackmail.'

★ ★ ★

When they leave the Studio Club the sky is still threatening, but the rain has let up a little. Tug turns east on Fountain, then north on Gower to Hollywood Blvd.

'I think she likes me,' says Tug.

'Who?' says Hallinan.

'What do you mean, who? Linda Kwan. Did you see the way she looked at me?'

'I wouldn't let it go to your head. I suggest a strong dose of saltpeter with your meals until this case is over.'

'You're no fun at all, big guy.'

'That's what Dorothy says.'

'How is Dorothy?'

'Gone. She wants a divorce.'

'Geez, Rusty. I didn't know you two were on the rocks. Maybe she's trading in a forty for two twenties.'

'You're a real sensitive guy, Tug. And it's forty-five.'

'So, who's counting? What do you make of Miss Kwan's story? Horst Kepler is certainly up to no good.'

'I know, but is he involved in the Adler girl's disappearance? The only thing he smuggled out of the party was the guest book, and he couldn't pull that off without getting busted by an old lady.'

'I ran him and he comes up clean,' says Tug, 'but sometimes things happen to kids that don't come out until years later.

They're threatened. They're afraid to talk.'

'You have a point. What we need to concentrate on is getting the film he took at the party and getting that guest book back. It's the most accurate record of who was there.'

Hallinan stretches his leg and rubs his bad knee.

'When is the doc going to operate? If the captain sees you gimping around, he'll stick you behind a desk.'

'When I lose twenty, maybe thirty pounds. I gotta get the weight off the joint or I'll screw it up again.'

'So, how you doing?'

'Great. I lost ten pounds and only put fifteen back on. You wanna go for pizza and beer after work?' Tug laughs.

They stop for traffic on Hollywood and Gower. A few blocks east, wind blows a lone figure down the boulevard. 'Take a right,' says Hallinan. 'I see someone I need to talk with.' There's only one person he knows who carries a frilly lavender umbrella.

Tug swings a right, their windshield

wipers set on low, their tires hissing over the wet pavement. Within a few blocks the Hollywood of swanky nightclubs and famous movie theaters is supplanted by ratty hotels, pawn shops and blue movie houses. The woman with the umbrella comes into sharper focus. She's wearing a silk scarf over her hair, spiky high heels, a lavender raincoat over black slacks, and a pink shoulder bag.

'Holy moly!' says Tug. 'I'd like to take that chassis for a spin around the block.'

Hallinan suppresses a smile. 'I can probably fix you up,' he says. 'Remember Tyrone?'

'What about Tyrone?' He looks at Hallinan's grin, then shakes his head. 'You can't be serious. He looks better than the date I took to the senior prom.'

'She goes by Tyrisse now, so don't embarrass her with any of your bullshit. She can get information from people who wouldn't even talk to us and be welcome in places where we couldn't get in the door.'

'All right, you don't have to beat me over the head.'

'You know the pastor of that skid row church off Main, does a lot of work with the poor?'

'Yeah, the Reverend Malcolm Dewberry, the big bag of wind who does that Sunday morning radio show.'

'He says Tyrisse and her girls are big contributors to their soup kitchen. When she's not giving money away, she volunteers in the kitchen.'

Tug shrugs nonchalantly. 'So what? She can afford it. She makes better money at Dark Desires than she ever would have teaching school. She makes more money than we do.'

'Stop the car, Romeo.' Tug swings to the curb. Hallinan rolls down the window. 'Hey, Tyrisse. Climb in the back and warm up.'

Ty delicately folds her umbrella and slides shivering into the back seat. 'Thanks, baby. I was freezing my buns off out there.' With black kid gloves on her hands and the bow of the scarf covering her throat, she looks like any other attractive lady walking down Hollywood Blvd. on a rainy afternoon.

A vehicle roars up beside them and slows with a squeal of brakes. Buzz Storch cranks his neck and peers into their car. Ty hunches into the collar of her coat, trying to look invisible. Someone behind them punches a horn and the Studebaker shoots on down the street, turning left at the next corner.

'That was Buzz,' says Tug. 'What the hell has gotten into him?'

Hallinan looks at Ty. 'It's okay. He's gone. Where's your car?'

'Getting the tires rotated. It won't be ready for another hour. A man offered to take me to lunch, then drive me back to the tire place, except he tried robbing me instead. Look what fell in the street when I jumped out at the light.' She reaches in her purse and hands Hallinan an expensive alligator wallet.

Hallinan flips it open. It's fat with cash, bills so crisp he can smell the ink. He peels off two one hundreds and presses them in Tyrisse's hand. 'For the soup kitchen,' he says.

'Thank you, sweetie.' She folds the money into her purse. 'That'll buy a lot of hamburger and mashed potatoes.'

'I didn't see that,' says Tug.

'It's the fine for ungentlemanly behavior,' says Hallinan. 'Besides, he can afford it. I saw his business card. The guy's a Beverly Hills psychiatrist.'

Tug laughs out loud. 'They're all a bunch of nutcases. You got a head problem, I say take it to Dear Abby and save yourself thirty-five bucks an hour.'

'Pull up to the mailbox,' says Hallinan. Tug looks in the rear-view. He eases to the curb and Rusty drops the wallet through the mail slot.

'What did you do that for?' asks Ty. 'I didn't even get his name.'

'That's the point. Next you'll be calling his wife and getting things all stirred up. Let's just stamp out the fuse and let it go at that.'

'I bet you'll let me light a fuse under Lobo Calderone.'

Hallinan snaps his head around. 'What about Calderone?'

'I was looking for a pay phone when you pulled up. On my way to the tire place I saw Caldrone go into the Crown

Royale with his girls. Cupcake was with him. She's got a black eye the size of an eggplant. He uses room 327 because it's closest to the back stairs.'

'The elevator still out in that dump?' asks Tug.

'That's right, baby.' The car lunges forward, throwing Tyrisse against the back of the seat. 'Watch your back, boys,' she says. 'Calderone doesn't go anywhere without a straight razor in his boot and a gun in his belt.'

7

Chaos at the Crown Royale

The Crown Royale has a reputation for prostitution, disorderly conduct, domestic assaults, rapes, murders, drug overdoses, and suicides . . . a full menu of violent misconduct and human folly contained in five stories, thirty dilapidated rooms per floor.

The building slumps in the rain. Stress fractures from the quake of '33 zigzag down its weathered brick façade, its torn window shades dating from the Coolidge administration. The only thing holding it together is a rusty fire escape bolted to the west wall of the building. Two wary hookers smoking in the entryway see them and duck inside the lobby.

'They made us,' says Hallinan. He turns to Ty. 'Your butt is not to leave that seat,' he says. 'You read me?'

'I'll just sit here and have a quiet

smoke,' she says.

'Let's do it,' says Tug. He's already out of the car, bolting into the lobby with its worn linoleum and sagging sofas. The building has a bad case of halitosis — stale nicotine, spilled booze, backed-up plumbing. The desk clerk's hand moves toward the switchboard. Tug looks at him with eyes like bullets. 'You touch that and I'll strangle you with the cords.' The man drops his hands and slides his chair back a few feet.

Tug hits the second floor landing, every step jolting the skeleton of the old building. Hallinan, handicapped by his bad knee, knows his part. He moves down the side of the building to the back exit, where Calderone is likely to attempt his get-away.

By the time Tug reaches the third floor, the alarm has been sounded throughout the building. Deadbolts click, drugs are flushed, marijuana smoke is waved out open windows. He doesn't care. The only thing on today's agenda is Lobo Calderone. By the time he reaches room 327, Lobo and his girls are flying down the back stairs to the alley.

From the back exit Hallinan hears the shrieks of the girls and the thud of Lobo's boots descending the stairs. He's waiting for the door to open, gun in hand, when he hears the clip of high-heeled shoes. Hallinan turns his head and sees Tyrisse coming around the corner of the building. 'Go back, damn it!' he shouts as she prances toward him.

The door explodes outward, knocking him sideways, the gun flying from his hand and skidding across the asphalt. Two girls carrying their shoes rush past him and disappear down the alley in their stocking feet. A third stumbles and falls, causing Calderone to trip over her. He sprawls on the wet concrete, but quick as a cat is back on his feet, straining to reach Hallinan's gun.

Hallinan lunges and gets to it first, feeling every ounce of his extra twenty — or is it thirty? — pounds. His hand is locked on the grip when Calderone's foot snaps out, his hard-soled boot slamming into Rusty's bad knee with crushing force.

Something rips beneath his knee cap

and he hollers in pain. As he goes down, a bullet from his gun spits skyward. He collapses on the ground and rolls on his side. There's no time to draw a steady bead on the fleeing figure, but he pulls off a shot in the general direction. Calderone scales a backyard fence and vanishes. The girl who'd been on the ground, her head covered with her arms, jumps up and takes off down the alley like a young gazelle.

'You winged him,' shouts Ty, her big hazel eyes bright with excitement.

'I don't think so,' moans Hallinan, clutching his wounded knee.

'Didn't you see how he dragged his leg over the fence?' She straightens her rain coat and reties her scarf.

'You okay?' Hallinan asks, unable to rise.

'Not really. I cracked the heel off my best pair of shoes.'

Tug blasts through the exit door and sees his partner on the ground.

'He's gone,' says Hallinan. 'He did a job on my knee.'

'I'll help you up, baby,' says Tyrisse.

'What the hell are you doing here?' screams Tug, his face bloated with rage. 'Don't you understand English? You were told to stay in the blasted car!'

'I was out of smokes. I was just . . . Rusty winged him, got him in the leg.'

Hallinan shakes his head. 'He scaled the fence like an Olympic high-jumper.'

'I ought to wring your neck,' says Tug, taking an aggressive stride toward Ty. She raises her hands defensively and hobbles backward on her uneven shoes.

'Let it go, Tug,' says Hallinan. 'It was my fault. What about Cupcake? The girls who ran out are the same ones I've seen around town for a couple years.'

'She's upstairs, roughed up a bit, but safe. She wants her mother.'

Hallinan groans as Tyrisse helps him wobble to his feet. 'Don't we all,' he says.

★　★　★

'You get yourself to the E.R., Hallinan,' says Captain Stanek. 'I've been pretending not to notice the bum knee for a couple months, but the jig is up.'

'But, sir . . . '

'Just do it, Lieutenant. I don't want you back on duty until you've been cleared by a physician.'

'Yes, sir.'

'I talked to a nurse at Hollywood Presbyterian. They're keeping Amanda overnight,' says Stanek.

'How is she doing?'

'How do you think she's doing? The official post-mortem on her husband won't be available until tomorrow, but the coroner says the body belongs to Chase. He'd been dead from the gunshot for a few hours before the car was set on fire.'

'So the Mexican kids are in the clear on the killing.'

'That would be my opinion.'

'Does Mrs. Chase have family in the area, someone to look after her?'

'Her parents are missionaries. They're down the Amazon teaching the savages not to eat one other.'

'They could have done that right here in L.A.'

* * *

After dropping Tyrisse at the tire place, Tug goes up the stairs to the Adler house while Hallinan broods in the car. When he comes back down he says nothing has changed in the Daisy Adler disappearance. No ransom calls have come in, and a mounted search party is scheduled for the morning. Hallinan reluctantly hands his partner the stack of flyers. Turning over his case is like having the core of meaning ripped from his life. His marriage has fallen apart, his body is a wreck, and now his career is on hold indefinitely.

'I'll get the media on it in the morning,' says Tug. 'Let me drive you to the E.R. I'll find a way to get your car back to the house.'

'I'm fine to drive. I'm fine, just fine.'

* * *

Late New Year's Day, Libra Gordy drives her motor home onto a bridle trail at the eastern end of Griffith Park. The rain has stopped, but the trees still drip liquid gold, backlit by the winter sunset. Libra is not beautiful by Hollywood standards, but she has a warm earthy appeal, a solid build with light freckled skin, a bushel-basket of curly red hair, and friendly brown eyes.

Her stepfather, Steven Bannister, died on the last Monday in December. Her stepbrother, Reginald, inherited the Beverly Hills estate and her stepsister, Sybil, the Arrowhead lodge. Libra received the deed to a piece of property her deceased mother had brought into the marriage and a monthly stipend just large enough to keep the wolf from the door. She was told the property is in the Mojave Desert in a place called Willow Shade outside the town of Dry Rock.

Libra's mother died several years ago and her biological father is blowing in the wind. All her mother remembered was that he had a dog named Harry and an old Ford . . . or was it a Chevy? She denied that it was a one-night stand. It was at least two nights and no one was standing. Her mom was trying to be funny, but it wasn't enough for a kid who needed real answers.

Libra had returned from Steven's funeral as the locksmith was leaving the Beverly Hills estate. Her stepsiblings had left her the registration and keys to the motor home, with the proviso she vacate the property within twenty-four hours.

The vehicle was packed with her possessions and her favorite books from Steven's library. None of this came as a surprise. She didn't like them. They didn't like her. They didn't even like each other.

Libra had seen a lot of disappointment in her 23 years. When she became pregnant at sixteen, her boyfriend, handsome, gentle Denny Sunquist, was sent away to a military academy where he died of appendicitis six months later. She was sent to the Catholic Home for Delinquent and Wayward Girls, just north of the Mexican border. 'Delinquent' translated to 'pregnant and unwed'. Her only crime had been falling in love and taking it a step too far.

The day after her little girl was born, Libra was told the child had died during the night. It was a lie. The Home was a baby-brokerage where mothers were young and helpless and newborns went to the highest bidder. Someone had her child. They would be rich, married and Catholic. Since that day she's looked for her little girl in every face of every child she sees.

★   ★   ★

As Hallinan waits in the E.R., the double doors fly open and a gurney squeaks into the room.

'We got a bleeder,' shouts one of the attendants. 'We applied a tourniquet but I think he exsanguinated at the scene.'

A doctor rushes over. 'Looks like a bullet severed the femoral artery,' he says. He presses a stethoscope to the man's chest.

'I wouldn't go to any extreme measures on his behalf,' says Hallinan.

'Who are you?' asks the doctor, taking a pen light from his pocket.

'Detective Lieutenant Rusty Hallinan, L.A.P.D.'

The doctor lifts the patient's eyelids one at a time and pierces the pupils with a stiletto of light. 'Fixed and dilated,' he says. He turns to Hallinan. 'You have something to do with this man's condition?'

'I thought I missed. Guess it's my lucky day.'

'You are one cold bastard, Hallinan.'

'He sells young girls to all comers for three bucks a pop. You tell me who the cold bastard is.'

The doctor ignores him. 'Where did you find him?' he asks the attendants.

'A woman found him in her backyard when her dog wouldn't stop barking.'

'Any I.D.?'

'Nothing on him.'

'His name is Geraldo 'Lobo' Calderone,' says Hallinan 'His life's journey is recorded on a rap sheet about three feet long. His family's written him off, so I guess that makes me next of kin.'

'You micks have a sick sense of humor.' He nods to the attendants. 'He's dead. Take him to the cooler.'

* * *

'Well, my man, you did it this time,' says Dr. Moisha Levinson, Rusty's orthopedic surgeon. He palpates the crushed pulp that was once a functional knee. 'Leave it to you to finish the job the Japs started.'

'Would you stop poking it?' Having returned from x-ray, Rusty sits on a cold exam table in a too-small hospital gown that, like all hospital gowns, doesn't close properly in the back unless you are a broomstick.

'We'll have to move your surgery date up. It's not just those leftover bits of shrapnel from the war. Now you have a badly torn meniscus.'

'Meniscus?'

'Cartilage. Puppet strings. Keeps joints from falling apart.' Levinson opens his autoclave and pulls out a syringe the size of a rolling pin.

'What's that for?'

'I'm going to aspirate fluid from the joint to relieve the pressure. It'll build up again, so I want you to call my office in the morning and make an appointment for Wednesday. Then we'll set a date for surgery.'

'Sorry, can't be done, Doc. I'm in the middle of a case.'

Levinson gives Hallinan an incredulous look. 'Everyone I see is in the middle of something, Rusty. When my Aunt Fanny died she had three pages to go in *Gone With the Wind*. She never got to hear Gable say he didn't give a damn. How unfair is that?'

'I'm serious, Moisha.'

'Just a little prick,' says Levinson, inserting the needle. The reservoir fills with bloody fluid. Hallinan feels dizzy. The doctor withdraws the needle. 'Feel better?'

'Not much.'

'I'll send you home with pain pills. Just don't take too many.'

'What's too many?'

'If you wake up in the morgue cut the dose in half.'

'You're a mensch.'

Levinson laughs. 'The instructions are on the bottle.' He removes his gloves with a rubbery snap and tosses them in the refuse container. 'How's the diet coming, old boy?'

'My scale's on the blink.'

'That bad, eh? The nurse will be in to

wrap the knee and bring you a set of crutches. I want you off your feet until I see you on Wednesday. Give my best to Dorothy.'

8

Amanda

After the nurse supplies crutches and pills, Hallinan rides the elevator to the third floor and badges the nurse behind the desk.

'Detective Hallinan for Amanda Chase,' he says.

'I thought you were a patient.'

'Just a bad day at the office.'

She laughs. 'Room 310. Two officers are with her now. Keep it brief. The patient needs her rest.'

He crutches his way down the hall. The pervasive smell of rubbing alcohol and antiseptic triggers memories of the sweltering, bug-infested field hospital in the Philippines. At the far end of the corridor Edwards and Conover step into the hall and head his way.

'She had something to do with this,' says Conover as they walk shoulder to

131

shoulder, voices lowered conspiratorially. 'For the first time in his life hubby takes the station wagon. It ends up torched. He ends up with a bullet in his head. She ends up with the Mercedes.'

'It's a BMW, not a Mercedes. I wouldn't let Gladys near my Chevy and it's got one hundred and fifty thousand miles on it,' says Edwards.

'It's the insurance angle that's going to break this case. All we have to do is follow the money.'

'Ever see the movie *Double Indemnity?*' says Edwards. 'What was Fred McMurray's famous line — ? 'I did it for money and I did it for a woman. I didn't get the money and I didn't get the woman.' Ain't that the breaks?'

'Hello, boys,' says Hallinan, leaning casually against the wall with a cigarette between his fingers.

'Jesus, what are you doing here?' says Conover.

'Visiting a sick friend.'

'You don't look any too healthy yourself,' he says. 'What the hell happened?'

'Remember Lobo Calderone?'

'What, you let him get the best of you again?' snickers Edwards.

'Only as far as the morgue. That's where he ran out of blood.'

Conover and Edwards have a good laugh until the nurse puts a finger to her lips. It's hard to look at Edwards without staring at the oozing black mole on his chin.

'You guys on missing person's detail?' Hallinan asks.

'Not since you and Boatwright got the juicy one on Fairbanks, but an H-187 fell in our laps.'

'A homicide?'

'Gunshot victim in Boyle Heights. He resided in Hollywood, so we're working side by side with Hollenbeck Division.'

'Any promising leads?'

'A gang of pachucos driving a stolen pickup were caught with the victim's plate,' said Conover. 'They may have done the dirty work, but we figure the wife's behind it.'

'How you figure that?'

'Give us a day or two. We're still digging.'

'Come on,' says Edwards. 'I need a

brewsky. Say hi to the Tugster. And congrats on icing Calderone.'

∗ ∗ ∗

Hallinan taps lightly on the door and swings into Amanda's hospital room. Her bed is next to the window, her face turned toward the dark pane and the lights of the city beyond. Her hair spills across the pillow and one slender arm rests on the white bedspread.

'Amanda,' he says quietly.

She turns with a wince of discomfort. He can see she's been crying, but she manages a smile. 'Detective Hallinan.'

'It's Rusty now, remember? How are you feeling?'

'A little tired, but I'll be fine.'

He arranges her pillow so she can sit up. She smells like rain-washed flowers, and the soft gold highlights in her hair make you want to touch it. He leans his crutches against the wall and sits in the chair near the head of the bed.

She looks at his bandaged knee. 'What happened?'

'An old injury is all.'

'It must be painful.'

'It's not so bad. While you were gone I borrowed your keys and checked out the BMW. There's no reason it can't be driven.'

'That's all the more bewildering, isn't it?'

Hallinan leans forward. 'Amanda, think. Do you have any idea who might have wanted your husband dead?'

'Gavin? He had no enemies. If you'd known him you'd understand. What I can't figure out is why he was in Boyle Heights. We don't know anyone there. Please tell me you're involved in the investigation.'

'I'm assigned to Missing Persons, but that doesn't mean I can't keep my ear to the ground.'

'I'd appreciate that. They're releasing me tomorrow. I'm dying to go home and sleep in my own bed.'

'Will you let me drive you home?'

'Thank you. I'd like that. I'll be ready to go around ten. You know, Rusty, I feel like I'm living a stranger's life. I want my own life back, the one with a husband and a baby on the way.'

*　*　*

Hallinan parks the Buick at the curb and sits looking up at his house. With no light in the windows and no Beezer waiting to savage his shoelaces, it takes on a desolate, almost abandoned air. Hallinan is the kind of man who needs someone to take care of. It's the way his dad was, the way he was raised. He's just never felt it as acutely as he does now. He'd wanted to take care of Dorothy, but she did a very good job of taking care of herself. Not being needed by the people you love is a very lonely feeling.

As Hallinan inserts the key in the front door, he feels a crunch beneath his feet. He pulls the pen light from his pocket and casts the beam downward. He's standing in a puddle of raw eggs. The gluey mess sticks to the threshold, yolks hardening on the screen door. He's puzzled for a moment, then a smile creeps across his face.

Dorothy. The switched locks.

'Gotcha!' he laughs, punching the air.

★ ★ ★

Daisy should have listened to Mom and let Teddy come back in the morning, but Sigrid put out cat food and that changed everything. A painfully thin coyote cleaned out the dish. When she rattled the French door, the animal cowered on its haunches, overturned the water bowl and vanished into the night.

She was about to crawl back in bed when Teddy appeared on the patio. She opened the door and tried to call him inside, but he scampered up the path behind the house. 'You little monster!' she scolded. 'Now you're in for it.' A coyote had killed the next door neighbor's cat and she didn't want anything bad to happen to Teddy even if he deserved it.

Daisy ran across the patio and scrambled up the path. She should have put on her robe, but she'd be back inside in a second or two. When she got to the top of the hill Teddy was nowhere to be seen. She took a

137

few small detours into the chaparral but soon her teeth were chattering. When something bigger than a cat crackled through the bushes beside the path she turned around and went back.

She climbed to the top of the rise and looked down at the pink house. No light came from the windows. No laughter. She wondered if Mom remembered to save her a piece of Dad's birthday cake. Strange, how things didn't look quite the same as they had before. In fact, there was no house. There was nothing but an empty hillside.

She couldn't be that far from home. She'd simply got turned around. Daisy called for Mom. She called for Sigrid. She felt in the pocket of her nightgown and her good-luck money was gone. For the first time in her life no one came running when she started to cry.

While the moon was still high, she began picking her way through the underbrush, hoping to find the path to the house. She'd been walking aimlessly for hours when the storm rolled in. She was dripping wet when she finally found a cavity beneath a rock ledge. Inside were empty beer cans, Chinese food cartons and a discarded tablecloth. She wrapped the tablecloth around her shoulders and spent the night shivering and listening to the rain.

9

Dorothy

Hallinan is sleeping when the key clicks in the front door and a cold draft whispers through the bedroom curtains. It isn't until the bed jiggles and a cold, wet nose presses against his eyelid that he wakes laughing. He is looking into the face of a little dog with big bright eyes and enormous bat ears.

'Beezer!' he says, as the rambunctious chihuahua races around the bed, jumping from pillow to pillow. He dives beneath the covers and nibbles Hallinan's toes with his sharp teeth. Unable to endure the toe-torture, he tosses back the covers and eases his legs over the edge of the bed. Beezer jumps up, licking and nipping his chin. Hallinan sweeps him into his arms and gives his sturdy little body an affectionate squeeze.

'I missed you too, buddy,' he says,

planting a kiss on Beezer's knobby head. A clatter comes from the kitchen accompanied by the slamming of cupboard doors.

'Oh, oh! Sounds like Cruella has arrived.'

He pulls himself slowly to his feet and hops to the bathroom, Beezer's toenails clicking on the hardwood as he prances in circles. Hallinan brushes his teeth and runs a wet comb through his hair. In ten minutes he's dressed and downstairs, bravely leaving his crutches behind. He leans against the kitchen door frame, his weight on his good leg.

'Dorothy, what a surprise.' She looks up from her crouched position, pulling pots and pans from the bottom cupboard. 'I must have missed the call announcing your arrival.'

'Don't be sarcastic,' she says, slamming the lid on a pot and dropping it into an already loaded cardboard box. 'Switching the locks was a clever move.'

'I thought so. You must have come to clean the eggs off my porch.'

'I'm sorry about that. I was having a bad day. My housekeeper is coming to clean up the mess.' Beezer paws at his dish, dancing and whining. Hallinan automatically reaches for the bag of dog food.

'He's eaten. If there's one thing I can't stand it's a fat dog,' says Dorothy. She means like his master but doesn't say it.

Hallinan hops over and fills the bowl. 'It's my house and my dog. Why are you here?' he says, watching Beezer dive into his kibbles, excitedly scattering half of them across the floor.

'Monty's kitchen is sadly ill-equipped. I'm taking the copper pans and leaving the stainless steel.' She loads the last of the cookware and wobbles slightly on her high heels as she pulls herself up. He instinctively touches her elbow to steady her ascent. 'I hope you've given some thought to those papers, Rusty. You can make this easy or hard, but it's going to happen either way.'

'You caught me off guard, Dorothy . . . your leaving me, I mean.'

'Then you're less observant than I thought you were.' She pauses, her voice slightly unsteady. 'Please, just sign the papers.' For a split second her brittle façade cracks and he sees genuine sadness beneath it.

'Okay, I'll talk with Father Pat at St. Francis,' he says. 'But I made no secret about my position on divorce before we tied the knot.'

'That celibate old goat!' she says, brushing away an angry tear. 'You already know what he's going to say.'

'You're not the only one with a reputation to protect. The guys at the station look up to me.'

'You mean that motley crew of fornicating alcoholics? Who the hell cares what they think?' She takes a couple deep breaths. 'Just give it some honest consideration,' she says. 'Do you mind carrying the box to the car?'

'I'm sorry, Dorothy. I reinjured my knee.'

She explodes. 'For crissake, Rusty, lose some weight!' Beezer gives a startled yelp as she sets him on top of the pots and pans and struggles with the box to the car. After she drives away Hallinan calls Tug at his apartment.

He barely gets out, 'It's me,' before Tug says, 'What did the doctor say?'

'I see him again on Wednesday. I'm going to try and get a release, at least until the Adler case is cleared.'

'Why do I smell the strong odor of bullshit?'

'Okay, I have a torn meniscus, but it's not a death sentence. What's on the day's agenda?'

'Nothing for you, big guy. The search is underway. The papers are on it. Strongbow will stay on the phones and Trudy and Linda have volunteered to plaster the city with flyers.'

'It's Trudy and Linda now?'

'It was their idea, so help me. Garner and I are checking the list of known sex offenders against Mrs. Adler's guest list.'

'While you're doing that, I'm going to hunt down Kepler. I want that guest book and I want all the film he shot at the party. That's just between you and me, okay?'

★　★　★

Balanced on crutches, Hallinan arrives at Kepler's studio around nine. He clatters through the door into a waiting room lushly carpeted in a rose-grey pile, artful black-and-white photos of celebrities covering the walls. A distinguished older woman in a grey suit and gold knot earrings looks up from her typewriter. Her name plate reads Dona Thatcher.

'Good morning, Miss Thatcher. I'm looking for Horst.'

'I don't expect him until the end of the day.'

'He must have gone straight to the shoot.'

'Yes, that's right.'

'I'm supposed to meet him, but it's my first time out there and the map he drew is a bit sketchy.' He shows her the flip side of the business card. 'He told me to turn off near a bar, but I can't read the name of the road.' Before he sets off on a wild goose chase, he wants to make sure that Kepler is in Chatsworth.

'Let me see,' she says. 'I've heard him mention Miners Gulch Road.'

'Thank you, Miss Thatcher. I remember now.'

'What's your business with Mr. Kepler? He seldom allows visitors on the set.'

'I'm on publicity for the upcoming release.' He has no idea what he's talking about, it just sounds like something a Hollywood big shot would say.

'Crown Enterprises does our publicity,' she says, looking over the top of her glasses. 'What did you say your name is?'

Hallinan is already crutching out the door. He clears the curb, tosses the crutches in the car and drops heavily onto the car seat. He drives away without looking back.

★ ★ ★

Hallinan checks his watch and heads for the hospital. Amanda rises from a chair by the window with a warm smile. It's been a long time since a woman smiled at him when he walked into a room. It feels like the sun rising after a long winter's hibernation.

'Hi, Rusty. I'm checked out and ready to go.' She wears grey wool slacks and a fluffy white sweater, looking painfully young without make-up and her hair pulled back in a ponytail. 'Last evening Mr. Hornsby let my friend Julia in the apartment so she could bring me some going-home clothes.' She picks up her raincoat from the back of the chair and puts an arm through one of the sleeves.

'Here, let me help you with that,' he says, taking hold of the coat as he juggles the crutches and drops one. He shakes his head. 'Sorry. It can only go downhill from here.'

She laughs and touches his cheek with gloved fingertips. The simple gesture sends a quiver through his body. 'I can do it,' she says, slipping effortlessly into the other sleeve, tying the belt and looping a bright silk scarf around her neck.

'Shall we?' she says.

He opens her car door when they get to the parking lot and drives toward the Castleton. 'I think you're terribly brave,' he says.

'Not really. I've simply put my breakdown on hold. The coroner called this morning. It's official now. The man in the car was my husband, so there's no more pretending. Aside from funeral arrangements, I have to cancel the purchase agreement on the Topanga Canyon house, maybe move to a smaller apartment.'

'What about life insurance?'

'Gavin suggested it a while back, but we were both so young and healthy, I thought we should wait a few more years. You never think something like this is going to happen.'

'Are you hungry? Would you like to go out for something to eat?'

'I think I need to go home and rest. Nights in the hospital aren't very restful, especially when they wake you up to give you a sleeping pill.'

'I see your point. Promise to call me if you need anything, anything at all.'

'What I need are answers, Rusty. I want to know who did this terrible thing to Gavin. When we know what he was doing in East L.A. we may find the answer.'

'You may be right. Are there relatives you can turn to?'

'My parents are in Brazil and I've never met my Wisconsin relatives. How about you, Rusty?' she says, redirecting the conversation away from herself. 'Do your parents live in L.A.?'

'My parents are the reason I work Missing Persons.'

'What do you mean?'

'Five years ago, almost six now, they left on vacation, Dad pulling a Silverstream with a Ford truck. They were off to see the Wild West, old mining towns and ghost towns where the gold and silver panned out. And fish. Mom and Dad loved to fish. They called me as they headed east toward Nevada. That's the last time I heard from them. I haven't even taken their names off the deed to the house. I'm still waiting for them to walk through the door, but I know they never will.'

'That's dreadful. What happened?'

'I wish I knew. They dropped off the face of the earth.'

'Were the vehicles ever recovered?'

He shakes his head and swings into the parking lot of the Castleton. 'Well, here we are.' Hallinan hands over her keys and writes his phone number on the back of his card. 'Take this. It's my home phone. Call me when you're ready for that breakdown. My knee might be a disaster, but I have a shoulder that was made for leaning on. Come on, I'll walk you up.'

She smiles. 'Under the circumstances I think you'd better stay put.' The wedding ring on his finger catches the light. She looks at him with those blue-green eyes and holds his gaze a moment longer than she should. 'You're a nice man, Rusty. I don't know how I'd have made it through these last few days without your help. I do wish you well.'

There is something sadly wistful about the way she says it; something so . . . final. He watches her walk up the stairs and go inside. Long after he's back on the road, the faint scent of perfume lingers in the car. A small pain he can't quite define twists in his chest.

* * *

Hallinan heads north toward Chatsworth, the vision of Amanda floating across the landscape of his mind. Living with Dorothy's constant disapproval has numbed his emotions. Feeling them reincarnate is a confusing mixture of exhilaration and uneasiness, like a sleeping limb reasserting itself. If only he was younger . . . better-looking . . . thirty pounds thinner . . . if . . . if . . . if.

He drifts onto the shoulder of the road and pulls back into his lane. *Keep focused, Hallinan. You have work to do*, he reminds himself. Kepler. The guest book. He drives through rolling green hills studded with oak trees and giant boulders, hills that will turn gold-grey in the summer heat and burst into flame at the kiss of a carelessly tossed match. He passes ranch houses and weathered barns, cattle grazing in pastures, and an occasional country store doubling as a post office.

He slows the car when Bud's Suds comes into view. Out front are four motorcycles, three horses tied to a hitching post, a knot of leather-clad bikers, and three cowgirls drinking beer and whooping it up. When he turns onto Miners Gulch Road, he sees their eyes tracking him in the rear-view mirror.

He's several miles back in the hills when a battered sign, decorated with decades of rust and buckshot dings, appears on his left. It reads: LUCKY GAMBLE MINE.

Hallinan downshifts and starts up the incline, his car rocking from side to side on the ruts. He's gone about a hundred yards when a yellow Caddy flies down the hill. He cuts sharply to the side of the road as the car blasts by. It scrapes its underbelly at the bottom of the hill and races toward the main road. He doesn't get the license number or see who's behind the wheel, but he has the impression there was more than one occupant.

He continues cautiously up the hill to the flat, not knowing what to expect when he gets to the top. A van with its doors open sits in front of the weathered building Linda had described. He pins the van between his car and a water tank at the base of a windmill.

Stiff and balanced on crutches, Hallinan approaches the vehicle. He leans into the driver's side and looks at the registration strapped to the steering column. It belongs to Horst Eric Kepler, his residence listed on Ivarene in the Hollywood Hills.

The interior of the cab has been ransacked.

Gas receipts, crumpled cigarette packs, a shaving kit and a few photography supply catalogues are scattered around the interior. Maybe he isn't the only person after the guest book. He approaches the building and pounds on the door. 'L.A.P.D. Open up.' It's eerily silent. 'I'm coming in.'

He pushes on the door and it squeaks open on rusty hinges. Mining equipment lines the walls, dust motes dancing in a shaft of sunlight streaming through the dusty windows. A mouse scurries across the floor.

Again he announces himself, opens a second door to his left and enters a room with high ceilings and open rafters. There's a movie set against the right wall, consisting of an ornate bed with a scarlet velvet backdrop. A man fitting Kepler's description lies naked on the mattress. His hands are bound to the headboard with pink stockings, his feet duct-taped to the footboard. An ice pick rises like a radio antenna from his chest. Beside the bed is a very expensive camera, at least it was before someone removed the film and smashed it to smithereens.

'God!' says Hallinan, blowing out his breath. His heart pounds in his chest. No matter how many times he looks at death, he never gets used to it. He's learned to accept it, to move beyond it, hopefully solve it, but he never gets used to the raw savagery of the homicide scene. He remembers what Kepler told Linda: 'It's not who you know. It's what you know about who you know.' Maybe the man knew one thing too many.

Hallinan approaches the bed. Kepler's undershorts are stuffed in his mouth, his wide eyes capturing for eternity the denouement of a life that has not ended well. Film cans have been opened and tossed on the floor, their contents burned and lying in melted clumps, as if the perpetrator or perpetrators wanted to obliterate the identity of whoever was on them. Hallinan is long on motives, but short on suspects.

And he has a problem. He's not supposed to be here, but with a gaggle of bikers and cowgirls watching him go up the road, he's lost the luxury of deniability. And what about Miss Thatcher? He can see her being questioned now. 'Any identifying characteristics, ma'am?' 'No, officer, just your average red-headed fat man on crutches.'

Back at Bud's, the bikers buy him a beer and tell him there were three guys in the Caddy who almost plowed into their bikes as they skidded across the intersection. They were too busy scrambling for cover to get the license plate number.

Hallinan calls the local sheriff and reports the homicide, then calls Stanek and brings him up to speed. He gives him Kepler's address on Ivarene.

'I've just about had it with you, Hallinan. I want a medical report on my desk in the morning. No more coloring outside the lines.'

10

An Unexpected Visitor

After an hour at the murder scene conferring with deputies from the sheriff's department, the forensic team arrives and Hallinan heads home. By the time he climbs the porch steps his knee is locked, the skin pulled tighter than an overstuffed sausage, a tom-tom throbbing in the joint.

All he wants is pain pills and a soft bed. As he pulls out his keys, a tall man steps from the shadows at the far end of the porch. He wears a ten-gallon hat, chaps with fringe as long as a horse's tail, and spurs with Spanish rowels that rattle when he walks.

'Hello, Monty,' says Hallinan wearily. He's seen Monty's face on a dozen magazines — big charismatic smile, blond curls, depressingly youthful and handsome. 'If you're here to kick the shit out of me, someone beat you to it.'

Monty looks genuinely offended. 'My mama would whoop me good if I took advantage of an aging man on crutches.'

Whoop me? Is this guy for real?

'It's nice to know the fellow who's enjoying my wife has such high standards,' says Hallinan.

'I know you're being sarcastic, but I'm only here at Miss Dorothy's behest. Seems we're both in love with the same woman, don't it?'

'Seems so. The only difference is you don't know what you're getting yourself into, kid. If you were smart you'd cut and run.' Hallinan reaches for his house key. 'My leg is killing me. If you want to talk you'll have to come inside.'

'I'll say my piece right here. It won't take but a minute.'

'You've got five, then I'm getting drunk and going to bed.'

'I want you to stop being pig-headed and sign those papers. If my parents find out I'm shacked up without benefit of marriage they're going to have a hissy fit, and I can't marry her as long as she's married to you.'

'Succinctly and accurately stated.'

'People in Wyoming are on the conservative side compared to you Hollywood folks, Mr. Hallinan.'

'Believe it or not, Monty, I'm on the conservative side myself. When I said 'until death do us part', they were more than idle words.'

'Then I will say just one thing and be gone. If your marriage to Miss Dorothy is all you hoped for when you walked down the aisle, all the more power to you. But if you're hanging on out of ego and spite, I intend to fight for her happiness and mine.'

True to his word, Monty tips his hat and drives away in a Lincoln with steer horns on the hood and spotted cowhide seat covers.

Hallinan lies in bed listening to the wind, the proverbial one-legged man in a butt-kicking contest. An aging man. He'd wanted Monty West to be an arrogant s.o.b. so he could feel good about hating him. Instead he's a likeable kid with a naïve streak as wide as . . . well, Wyoming. He washes down a handful of knockout pills with a shot of brandy and dreams that Horst Kepler died channeling Jack Webb through the ice pick in his chest.

★ ★ ★

There is no bullshitting Dr. Moisha Levinson, no drive-through surgery on tap, no jumping back in the saddle like you-know-who.

'Do you know you have a hundred-and-three fever, Rusty?'

'Maybe that's why I'm so lightheaded, Doc.'

'You've been staying off your feet, right?'

'Absolutely.'

'The meniscus is not only torn, now the knee is seriously infected. I'm sending you home with antibiotics. When the inflammation subsides, we'll fit you into the surgery schedule.'

'How soon before I'm back on the job?'

'Provided we don't cut the leg off?' Hallinan goes silent. 'I'm joking, but you have to stay off your feet and think salad instead of pizza. You're going to need

T.L.C. If Dorothy has vacation time coming, I suggest she take it now.'

* * *

When morning comes, hunger drives Daisy from her lair. It's still raining, but winter rains often last a week, so she doesn't have the luxury of waiting for it to clear. She wraps herself in the table cloth and begins walking.

Lightning flickers above Mt. Lee and thunder rumbles over the hills. There are houses in the distance, but canyons, steep hillsides and thick brush make it impossible to get to them. She calls for help, but everyone is indoors and she can't be heard above the clatter of the storm.

The tablecloth drags on the ground, becoming muddy and waterlogged. She stumbles on it and casts it aside. Mud sucks off a slipper and she keeps going. When her bare foot becomes bruised and raw, she switches the remaining slipper from foot to foot. Soon both feet are so sore it's hard to trudge on. She finds an abandoned ice chest on the hillside, hoping to find something useful inside. Except for an old candy wrapper, it's empty. Hours later, when she stumbles on it a second time, she knows she's been walking in circles.

Daisy is cold and hungry. Her hair hangs in wet strands over her face. Her lips and fingertips are blue and her face and body are full of scrapes and scratches. Horst wants her to look like a fluffy little kitten for the camera, not like something the cat dragged in. He's going to be very angry. He calls her his little gold mine, but never when Mom is around.

That afternoon the rain stops and the temperature plunges. When dusk comes she knows she'll have to survive another night in the cold. All she can think about is food, a warm bath and her own little bed. She finds a discarded piece of canvas from a tent. It's wet and smells moldy, but when evening comes she wraps it around herself and crawls beneath a hollow log. She's surprised when heat builds up inside her cocoon. She wonders if anyone is looking for her. She wonders how much trouble she's in.

In the distance, she sees the lights of the observatory. The building looks like a ship floating on a dark and distant sea. Daisy knows it's to the east. When morning comes, she'll walk in the direction of the rising sun.

★ ★ ★

Hallinan puts the medical report from Dr. Levinson on Stanek's desk. 'I hate putting you on ice, Hallinan, especially in the middle of a case,' he says.

'Conover told me that they've got suspects in the Gavin Chase homicide.'

'The Mexican kids? They stole the truck in front of a 24-hour convenience store at 3:15 a.m. The time is corroborated by both the clerk and the owner of the truck. By the time they got to the abandoned gas station Chase had been dead for hours just like the coroner said.'

'So, we're back to square one.'

'Yes and no. A witness walking his dog on the night of the shooting has come forward. He heard what he thought was a firecracker around midnight. He didn't realize until later that it was a gunshot. He saw a tall man in dark clothes and a western hat drive away from the scene in a blue-and-white coupé. It backfired and black smoke poured out of the tail-pipe.'

'Are Conover and Edwards still trying to implicate Mrs. Chase?'

'They're looking for an easy solve, but unless they find an insurance policy there's nothing to go on. She wasn't cheating on her husband. They were never heard arguing. From all accounts they were a happy, upwardly mobile young couple.'

'Find anything interesting in the Ivarene house?'

'Someone got there before I did. There was no guest book, and all the porn reels the neighbors said were kept on a shelf in the den were gone.

'How about a connection to the yellow Caddy?'

'We're looking into it.' Hallinan has the impression they aren't going to look terribly hard. 'Now, get out of here,' he says. 'I don't want to see you again until all of your moving parts have been repaired.'

11

Crossed Destinies

On her first night of freedom, Libra sleeps well in the new motor home. She drifts off to the hooting of owls and the haunting music of coyotes. Waking to a cold, ceramic-blue sky and red-tailed hawks circling above the hills, she makes coffee, dresses in a jeans outfit and tennis shoes, and walks down the bridle trail into the park.

She sits on a stump and closes her eyes. The sun climbs the sky, backlighting her flaming red hair and melting tension from her shoulders. Far to the west she hears the snorting of horses and the baying of hounds. When she opens her eyes she lets out a startled gasp, jumps up and spills hot coffee on her shoe.

A tattered little waif comes out of the chaparral in a shredded nightgown and one muddy slipper. Her hair is tangled

164

with burrs, her body covered with scratches and bruises. She looks abused and abandoned.

'Judas Priest on roller skates!' cries Libra, jumping to her feet and letting out a laughter-tinged sob. The child has her father's unmistakable golden hair and big blue eyes. 'My God, what have they done to you?'

'I'm lost,' says the little girl, bursting into tears. 'I want to go home.'

'Of course you do, Little Bean.' Little Bean. That's what Libra's mother called her when she was small. It pops out of her mouth as if it had been waiting all these years to be said. 'Mama Bear has been looking for you since the day you were born.'

'You have?' Daisy isn't sure what the lady means, but she's too cold and hungry to care. She's just glad to be found.

'Of course I have,' she says, throwing her cup in the bushes and sweeping the child into her arms. Her body is like ice and she is ghostly pale. Her hair is damp, her nightgown wet, and her scalp crawling with ticks. She looks like an orphan from the pages of *Oliver Twist*.

As Libra walks up the path with the child's tears falling on her shoulder, her weight feels natural and familiar in her arms. She fills an empty, lonely spot in her heart that nothing else in the world can fill. 'These are the last tears you will ever have to cry,' she says, giving Daisy an affectionate squeeze.

★　★　★

Two hours later, bathed and fed, the ticks and burrs removed, and her hair soft and clean, the little girl, who will answer to the name Bean, sleeps in a clean T-shirt in a cozy bed in the back of the motor home.

Bear takes the tattered nightgown and ruined slipper, walks half a mile down the path into a remote area of the park and tosses them deep into the chaparral. Half an hour later the motor home is speeding east toward the Mojave Desert.

★　★　★

In Dry Rock, California, population fifty, Libra pulls into the dusty lot of the Last Chance Café. Last chance for food. Last chance for gas. Last chance to use a dirty restroom before you hit the Nevada state line.

The screen door slaps against the frame behind them as they step inside, Daisy in a cute sun suit that is part of the wardrobe Libra bought her in Barstow. A swamp cooler in a side window sounds like wrenches being tossed in a cement mixer, and flies who can't find cemetery plots on the fly-paper hanging from the ceiling buzz lazily around the room, knocking their heads against the front window. An elderly waitress with a serious curvature of the spine and dyed orange hair moves around the room filling coffee cups. A Chinese cook with a waist-long queue flips burgers on the grill.

Five or six customers sit around eating and chewing the fat. An old buzzard with a spotted hound at his feet puts his empty plate on the floor. The dog rises with a labored groan and licks it clean. The waitress, whose name tag reads Millie, picks up the plate and carries it to the kitchen. Libra makes a mental note that it's blue with a chipped edge, and hopes it doesn't reappear bearing their food. She lifts Bean onto a stool at the counter and takes the one to her right.

'What'll it be?' says the waitress, returning from the kitchen and nodding toward the menu on the chalkboard. 'The milkshake machine is broken and we don't serve the round steak until five.'

'How does a hamburger and coke sound?' Libra asks Bean.

'It sounds good.'

'Millie,' says Libra, when their food arrives, 'we're looking for a town called Willow Shade, but I'm beginning to think it doesn't exist.'

'That's because it's a ranch, not a town, which would make you Libra Gordy.'

Libra is astonished. 'How can you possibly know that?'

'Steven Bannister called Zeke a couple weeks back. The good news was that he was on his deathbed. The bad news was that he was leaving you two thousand acres of sand, cactus and rattlesnakes. The creek running through it is the only thing that keeps it from being totally worthless. Water is everything around here, you know.' She turns to the old man with the dog. 'Zeke, get over here and meet your new boss. Zeke keeps the roofs from caving in and the cows from running off.'

Ezekiel walks over with his dog. He has long white hair pulled back in a rawhide tie and wears overalls, cowboy boots and a western hat with a rattlesnake band, the rattles and head intact, the fangs as sharp as hypodermic needles.

'You're looking good,' says Ezekiel, shaking Libra's hand. 'Got your mother's red hair. I haven't seen you since the day she took off with Steven. You couldn't have been more than six months old. I keep the snake population down on the place. Sell the skins. I been bit ten times and the snake died every time.' Libra thinks it's probably an oft-told tale, but everybody in the room laughs. Zeke looks over at the little girl sitting next to Libra. 'Yours?'

'Yes, that's Bean.'

'You like dogs, Bean?' he says.

'Yes, I do.'

'Well, this here is Ticky. He's fifteen years old. That's one hundred and five in dog years. You like my hat?' She nods and he leans over. She reaches out to touch the snake's nose. 'Boo!' he says. Bean screams with delight and pulls her hand back, laughing. 'I can see we're going to get along just fine. I'll let you girls eat your lunch in peace. Then you can follow me out to the ranch.'

As they tail Zeke's pickup through the desert, Bean tugs at Libra's sleeve. 'When are you going to take me home? I don't want to get in trouble.'

'You won't get in trouble, baby. Nobody cares if you take a little vacation with Bear. If you like the ranch they might even let you stay on.'

* * *

Winter drags on with no progress in the Gavin Chase homicide. Amanda often stands by the window looking at the rain, no longer sure what or who she is waiting for. At first she imagined Gavin coming

170

through the door with the blueprints for the Spanish house and a head full of big plans. As time passes his image begins to fade and she starts thinking about Rusty Hallinan and how much she wants to see him again. Maybe, if she wishes hard enough, she can wish the wedding ring off his finger. It's not a very honorable notion, but it's an honest one.

Hallinan hears from Tug less often now that the leads have dried up in the Daisy Adler case. Tug is dating Linda Kwan. Sigrid is back in Sweden. Gifts appear in Daisy's room on her seventh birthday. Helen soldiers on and Nathan holes up in his den. He broods. He forgets appointments with important celebrities. People talk. His patient load dwindles.

Hallinan and Dorothy are at an impasse. She keeps Beezer. He holds the papers hostage. *The Devil Wore Spurs* is a wrap and Monty signs on for his next role. During his recuperation from surgery, not a day goes by that Hallinan doesn't think about Amanda. When the phone rings he wants it to be her, but it never is.

When the chips are down, the only person who doesn't forget him is Tyrisse. She comes by the house with brandy, hero sandwiches and more Hollywood gossip than *L.A. Confidential*. She jokes around and calls him her fiancée. She keeps the conversation upbeat, but under all the sass and brass she fears Buzz Storch like a child fears the bogeyman. Her car has been broken into. Her room has been tossed. Hallinan concludes that she's got something Storch wants and she's not giving it to him. She plays her cards close to her chest and tells him the less he knows, the safer he is.

★　★　★

On the other side of town, Crystal Monet lives in fear. Cesar is quite open about having killed Gavin, but being privy to that kind of information is the sort of thing that can get you killed. When Cesar isn't with her, she's being watched by Old Tom or one of the bouncers. If she's dying, Cesar thinks she's taking too long to get the job done.

12

Starting Over

June, and the sun opens like a flower in a soft kiss of blue sky. In cut-off jeans, flip-flops and a T-shirt with a pink heart on the front, Amanda moves the BMW close to the water spigot and goes to work with her car-wash kit.

She's found a job typing and filing at a real-estate brokerage on Wilshire Blvd. She faithfully pays her rent and bills, but can't manage the BMW loan no matter how tightly she budgets. The dealership refuses to let her trade down to something affordable, so she's stopped making payments and waits anxiously for the vehicle to be repossessed.

In the noonday heat the sudsy water is cool and refreshing as it runs down her arms. She has a honey-dipped tan and her hair, now summer-blonde, is caught in a heart-shaped barrette at the nape of her neck.

After buffing the car to a mirror shine she starts on the interior. Amanda scoops everything from the glove compartment into a shoe box — mileage records, junk mail, matchbooks, restaurant menus. She whisks a few pennies and a stray pearl earring from under the seat and adds them to the collection. A shadow falls over her shoulder. Startled, she hits her head on the underside of the dash.

'A bit jumpy are we?' It's Dack Traynor with a cigarette dangling from his mouth, the pack rolled into his sleeve. She wonders how long he's been standing there watching her.

'Dack, what are you doing here? You know Mr. Hornsby took out a restraining order against you.'

'I'm broke. Gail's letting me crash on the couch. It's not like I'm actually living here.'

'I thought you were tending bar at the Monkey House.'

'The owner's wife came on to me and got me fired.'

Same old Dack.

Dack's eyes wander lustfullly over Amanda's body. Every rejection, however polite, intensifies his desire to drag her off by her hair and take what he wants . . . what he's wanted for a very long time.

'I can't talk right now, Dack,' she says, turning away from him. She leans down and whisks under the driver's seat. Something flies out of the car and lands at Dack's feet. He bends over and picks up a pink business card. 'Give that to me,' she says, leaning her elbow on the car seat. 'I'm not throwing anything away until I have a chance to go through things.'

He examines both sides of the card. 'You sure you want it?' he smirks. 'Maybe your husband wasn't the goody-two-shoes he pretended to be.'

She stands up, her hand extended. Her expression makes him wonder what she's capable of. A slap in the face? A jab in the eye? A knee to the family jewels? 'Give it to me, Dack, or I'll tell Mr. Hornsby.'

'You'll be s-o-r-r-y,' he says, placing the card in her hand. 'Before you throw it out, drop it in my mail slot. I can use a little excitement in my life.' She tosses it in the shoe box without looking at it and watches him strut away, leaving an unsettled feeling in the pit of her stomach.

*   *   *

Summer comes to Willow Shade, with its two old houses, weathered barns and corrals. There's a rock garden with a buckboard displayed among the cactus, a wagon wheel, rusty license plates, antique whiskey bottles and a steer skull. Bear and Bean live in the four-room house, Ezekiel in the bunk-house with the attached tool shed. The pale aqua skies are as high and wide as an ocean, and a carpet of red and yellow wild flowers rolls to the distant horizon.

On hot afternoons Bear and Bean swim in the creek and picnic along the bank. Bean wears jeans and little cowboy boots, beads and feathers woven into her braids. On her seventh birthday Uncle Ezekiel bought her a pony to ride around the corral. To a child, a week is a month and a month is a year, and 'those other people' in the pink house recede from memory like mist in a long-ago dream.

Bean loves being in Bear's comforting presence. On baking day Bear smells like vanilla and sugar. When she fires up the stove on chilly mornings, wood smoke hangs in her clothes. If her hands smell like onions there will be beef stew or chili for dinner. After dark she reads Bean adventure stories by Albert Peyson Terhune and James Oliver Curwood.

One evening Bear tells Bean that she is her real mother. She takes the photo of a handsome boy from her trunk and says he was her father who died before she was born. Bean doesn't look like Bear, but she is the image of the boy in the photograph. Bean doesn't know what to think. There are times she thinks Bear is confused, but she's confused too.

Early one morning Ezekiel trots his mare up to the house. Rustlers had cut their wire fencing and made off with two calves. He'll have to drive all the way to Crazy Horse to file a report at the sheriff's office.

'Can I come along?' says Bean, still

sleepy-eyed and in pajamas.

'No, you sit here and eat your pancakes. It's gonna be over a hunnerd out there. Tell you what, I'll stop at the general store on the way back and bring you a bag of candy corn.'

★　★　★

A cloud of dust rolls over the roof of the sheriff's office as Ezekiel pulls into the lot. The truck's cab smells like dog breath, the old man's jeans sweat-glued to the seat.

Sheriff Akin is snoring in his chair, feet propped on his desk, his face directed toward the fan. He's jowly and fat-bellied and ornery with the heat. The deputy turns from the front window. He's a tall, fit half-breed who's changed his name from Many Scalps to Grey Stoneacre, after a hero in a western novel. He hopes the change will garner votes when he runs against his boss in the next election.

'Sheriff, we got company,' says Stoneacre. He resists the urge to sweep Akin's feet to the floor. If things go his way on election day, he'll sweep him out the door. 'Amos, wake up!'

'What?' The sheriff opens his eyes.

'It's Ezekiel Bridger, the rattlesnake man.'

Ezekiel comes through the door with the hound at his heels, a blast of hot air lifting the edge of the wanted posters on the corkboard. Both man and dog look done in. Stoneacre brings the man a glass of ice water and a bowl of water for his dog.

'Thank you,' says Ezekiel. 'That's right considerate of you.'

'Miserable day to be out in this heat, Mr. Bridger,' says Akin, hoping the visit won't require him to get out of his chair.

'Two more calves gone missing last night, Amos. It's the second time in three months we been ripped off.'

'Probably coyotes, Ezekiel.'

'Not unless they drive a pickup truck.'

'I can take a report, but there ain't much we can do about it, is there Stoneacre? By now they're across the border on some Mexican's dinner plate.'

Stoneacre considers the question, although it wasn't intended to elicit a response.

'They leave any tire tracks, Mr. Bridger?'

'Yes indeed. There was a pickup and a horse trailer involved.'

'The molds I took last time are in the back. I'll drive out tomorrow and see if we have a match. The stock may be across the border, but I'm betting the thieves are local boys.'

'Thank you, Deputy St . . . ' Brakes screech on the road out front and there's a tremendous thud. Ticky trembles and crawls under the chair.

'What the hell . . . ?' says Akin, swinging his legs to the floor and almost knocking the fan off the desk.

Stoneacre flies out the door, Akin close behind. A flatbed carrying hay bales lies on its side across both lanes of traffic. A horse is down and struggling to rise, the leg of an unconscious boy pinned beneath him. The truck driver stumbles out of the cab and drops wailing to his knees.

'It's the Regan boy!' Akin shouts to Ezekiel from the doorway. 'Doc Jackson's number is in the file.' After Ezekiel summons the doctor, he dials the large-animal vet. The phone is still ringing when he hears a pistol shot and hangs up. He puts his head in his hands, his heart ticking like a broken clock. When he looks up, the photo of a little girl looks back at him from a flyer on the cork board.

Daisy Marie Adler. DOB 3/7/50
Blonde Hair. Blue Eyes.
Missing From Los Angeles. 1/1/57

The child would be seven now. She looks so much like Bean, they could be identical twins . . . or . . .

A ripple of apprehension travels up Ezekiel's spine. Steven Bannister never mentioned a granddaughter, but then he seldom talked about anything unrelated to money. Once the unthinkable pops into the old man's head, there's no getting rid of it. He goes to the corkboard, picks out the tacks, folds and pockets the poster along with two others to make the object of his interest less obvious. He whistles for Ticky, who crawls out from under the chair.

When he reaches his car the youth is being loaded into the ambulance. The sheriff removes the bridle from the dead horse and Stoneacre is taking the truck driver's statement.

No one notices as he hoists Ticky into the cab. 'I just wanted to report a theft and buy a bag of candy corn and now look,' he tells the dog. He dodges the bales of hay on his way out of the lot and heads toward home.

* * *

Amanda empties the odds and ends from the shoebox onto the bed, picks out the pearl earring and tosses it in her jewelry box. Among the junk mail, she finds unopened statements from Gavin's doctor. They cover September and October of the previous year, but she is only aware of the one visit he had in September with their family doctor. She doesn't know if there had been an outstanding balance at the time he was killed. She'll call the clinic on Monday.

The pink card lies in the bottom of the box. She picks it up and reads the print on the front.

CLUB VELVET
Featuring
'BODY BEAUTIFUL'
CRYSTAL MONET

She turns it over. On the other side is a message penned in a flourish of peacock-blue ink.

GAV: HE'LL BE AWAY ON WEDNESDAY
   NIGHT.
SAME TIME. SAME PLACE.
CRYS.

Gav? Crys? Same time? Same place?

The card is undated. Had Gavin been seeing another woman? She remembers Julia's words on the night of the party and how she laughed it off. But this is no joke. Maybe Gavin hadn't been the angel she thought he was. She doesn't welcome one more complication in her life. She should have let Dack keep the card.

At the bottom edge, in small print, is the address of the club: 66620 Clapton Road. She goes to the desk for a street map and spreads it out on the bed. Clapton is across the Los Angeles River in East L.A., the area known as Boyle Heights. The gas station where Gavin's car was found is three miles west of the club. Could there be a connection between Crystal Monet, Club Velvet and Gavin's murder? Amanda refolds the map. If she tells Conover and Edwards about her discovery, she'll be handing them the motive they need to arrest her — jealousy over another woman. Maybe she'll do a little snooping of her own.

* * *

Dack leans against the railing outside Amanda's apartment. He's memorized every word on the pink card. Amanda always acts so superior. Maybe this will knock her down a peg or two. He's dying to know what her next move will be. Whatever it is, he's going to be on her tail like fleas on a dog.

* * *

Irene Wickersham and her husband Harry sit reading in their comfortable front room in Echo Park, Harry going over the actuarial tables for his insurance brokerage, and his wife buried in a supermarket tabloid.

'Harry, listen to this,' she says.

'Don't bother me with that tripe, Irene. It'll rot your brain.'

'You'll want to hear this, Harry. It's an article about L.A.'s unsolved murders.' He looks at her over his spectacles, the lamplight reflecting off his bald spot. 'Remember that young architect fellow you were telling me about, the one who took out the big policy on his life? Double indemnity, wasn't it?'

'Gavin Chase. What about him?'

'He was murdered on New Year's Eve. Someone put a bullet in his head and burned his car.'

'What? Let me see that,' he says, putting his ledger aside and rising from his chair. He walks across the shag rug and snatches the tabloid from her hands. 'I don't know how this slipped past me,' he says. 'The widow never put in a claim.'

'That's unusual, isn't it, Harry?'

'Highly unusual.' He studies his wife's

face. 'If something happened to me, you'd put in a call a day or two after the funeral, wouldn't you, Irene?'

'Of course I would, dear. Perhaps even sooner.'

13

Scare Tactics

Rusty Hallinan walks through the moonlit garden behind his house. It's good to be back on the job. He's cut down on his smoking. He's eating healthier. He's lost twenty pounds. Stars flame over the rooftops on Sandalwood Street, the air scented with ripening oranges and night-blooming jasmine. He stops beside a profusion of purple flowers along the path. There's something about those blossoms that triggers a bittersweet sense of longing. He's reminded of a rainy day . . . a cup of coffee . . . Amanda and the scent of lavender in her hair. A million memories, kept under lock and key, come rushing back.

A persistent mosquito buzzes his ear and Hallinan goes inside. He sits down at the dining-room table and spreads the divorce documents in front of him.

Dorothy has Beezer, the piano and Monty. He has the stainless-steel cookware and a big lonely house. He signs beside the red exes and returns the pages to the envelope. He removes his wedding ring and seals it inside. Monty was right. Maybe he is hanging on for ego and spite. He'll give Dorothy the news as soon as she returns from Sedona where they're shooting Monty's latest western. She's moved on without a backward glance. It's time for him to do the same.

Deep in the night Hallinan wakes to the sound of rain. Lightning spikes through the clouds and thunder rolls softly across the rooftops. A woman stands at the window backlit by a storm-shadowed moon. There's a vague hint of lavender in the air. Hallinan pulls himself up on the pillows. The house shudders in the wind. A pane rattles in the sash. The phantom flutters in the draft from the staircase, her translucent image glowing like a candle in a gold glass bottle.

'This isn't really happening, is it?' he says.

'It's real if you want it to be, Rusty.'

She reaches out a hand as transparent as moonlight. When their fingers touch there's a snap of electricity and he wakes, staring into the empty darkness.

★   ★   ★

Amanda puts on a tailored navy-blue suit, white silk blouse and pearl earrings. She pulls her hair off her neck and fastens it with a butterfly clasp. She knows she dreamt last night, but the dream was like a message in a bottle that floated away when she opened her eyes.

She spends the morning typing real-estate documents and answering phones. Her boss is pleased with her work performance and she gets along well with clients and co-workers alike. Today, instead of having lunch with the girls, she rushes to Dr. Fraley's office three blocks away and pushes through the double glass doors into the waiting room. It's a relief to walk from the brutal noonday heat into the air-conditioned building.

'How may I help you?' asks the receptionist.

189

Amanda spreads the bills in front of her. 'I found these bills in my husband's car and I'd like to know if they've been paid.'

'These are from last year.'

'Yes, I know.'

The receptionist walks to a metal cabinet and pulls Gavin's file. 'Here we go.' She sets it on the counter and flips through the pages. 'Good news, Mrs. Chase. There's no outstanding balance. Except for the first appointment in September, paid with his card, the others he paid in cash.'

Amanda knows nothing of the October visits. 'Oh yes, now I remember. Dr. Fraley was treating him for anemia, I believe.' The receptionist gives her a questioning look.

'Wouldn't it be easier to ask Mr. Chase?'

'It's not a complicated question.'

'I think you need to talk with the doctor. He'll be back from lunch at two.'

Amanda looks at her watch. 'I've got to get back to work. If I call on my coffee break, can you get him on the line?'

'I'll do my best.'

Amanda makes it back to the office with three minutes to spare. On her break she uses the phone at the corner drugstore.

'Dr. Fraley here, Mrs. Chase.'

'Yes, Dr. Fraley. Thank you for taking my call. All I need to know is what you were treating my husband Gavin for.'

'Mr. Chase hasn't been my patient since October of last year when I referred him to Dr. Margolin.'

'He's never mentioned Dr. Margolin. Are you sure we're talking about the same person? Gavin Lee Chase.'

'I wish I could help you, but your husband is no longer my patent. You need to talk to Margolin.'

'But it . . . '

'I have to get back to my patients. Goodbye, Mrs. Chase.'

Margolin has an office in Beverly Hills. She dials his number. A man from the janitorial service answers. 'Dr. Margolin is on vacation, señorita. Call back in two weeks, *por favor*.'

'Thank you,' she says. What now?

When she returns from her break, line

one is blinking. She transfers the call to the proper party and when she looks up, Detectives Conover and Edwards are standing in front of her desk. They wear sweat-wrinkled brown suits and wilted ties loosened at the collar. Her heart gives a sharp jolt.

'What are you doing here?' she says. 'Is something going on with my husband's case?'

'Please stand up, Mrs. Chase,' says Conover.

'Why?' Bewildered she looks from face to face.

Edwards walks behind her and jerks her from the chair. He pulls her arms behind her back and snaps handcuffs on her wrists. His hand brushes roughly across her breasts, tearing a button off her blouse and revealing an inch or two of lacy bra. In front of the startled eyes of her boss and fellow workers she's pushed into the elevator. They drag her across the lobby and shove her into the back seat of an unmarked car.

★　★　★

The day is sweltering. A brown cloud of 3-pack-a-day smog is trapped in the Los Angeles basin. People on the street breathe through handkerchiefs and wipe their watering eyes.

Hallinan and Tug are going over the recent missing person's files when Stanek walks over. 'A hiker left a paper bag at the desk containing a child's nightgown and slipper. It was found off a remote trail in Griffith Park. The gown is a rag, but it could be the one Daisy Adler was wearing the night she vanished.'

Hallinan jumps to his feet. 'I want to talk to him.'

'I'm afraid he got away without giving his name.'

Half an hour later Hallinan and Tug are driving up Fairbanks Drive, dress shirts sticking to the car seats. 'I hate this part of the job,' says Tug. 'Those clothes are as good as a death certificate.' They pull the car into the shade in front of the Adlers' garage and get out, Hallinan with the evidence bag. Water pools beneath the urns in the shady corners at the edge of the steps as they climb to the front door.

The big tiger cat is lounging in the sun on the balcony wall. He gives them a golden-eyed glance, flexes his paws and goes back to sleep.

Helen Adler opens the door. She wears a whisper-blue summer dress. Her complexion has taken on a yellow pallor and her ankles are badly swollen. 'Let's go downstairs where it's cool,' she says. They follow her to the dining room and sit around a large oak table. The floor is covered with Spanish tiles, and a pair of French doors let in a cool breeze from the shaded patio.

'Would you boys like something cold to drink?'

'Thanks, but we're fine,' says Hallinan. 'If Dr. Adler is in, I think he should join us.'

'As soon as you called he had the urgent need to flee. He's the resident ghost, still pining after that young Swedish girl.' Helen looks at the bag in Hallinan's hand. 'I imagine you have something to show me. We might as well get it over with.'

'A hiker in the park found a few articles

of clothing that might be associated with your daughter's case,' says Hallinan. 'Are you ready to see what we have?' She nods and he sets the fragments of cloth in front of her.

She fingers the shred of slipper, bleached white from the elements, then sets it aside. She presses the tattered nightgown to her cheek. 'Daisy always smelled like baby powder after her bath. I can't smell it anymore.' She runs her fingers over the faded strawberry decorations. 'Yes, Lieutenant. There's no doubt. These were Daisy's.'

'I'm so sorry. Can I call someone to stay with you, Mrs. Adler?'

'Thank you, Lieutenant, but I think I'd like a few moments to myself. I'll call Sarah when I've collected my thoughts. I'd like to thank you both for all you've done on our behalf.' No one says it in so many words, but they believe that all they'll ever find of Daisy Adler are scattered bones among the chaparral.

'How does she do it?' says Tug, as they head back down the hill. 'I worry about people who hold it in like that.' They cruise in silence past houses set behind high walls covered with Bougainvillea and honeysuckle, fountains bubbling in the center of circular drives and sprinklers pulling rainbows out of the sunshine.

'Have you seen Ty lately?' asks Hallinan.

'Not for a while.'

'I haven't either. That worries me.'

*　*　*

Back at the stationhouse, Edwards crosses the parking lot as Tug and Hallinan get out of their car. 'I was right all along,' he says, barely able to contain himself.

'You mean your mother really is a hooker?' laughs Tug.

'Very funny. I'm talking about Amanda Chase. We found a policy. Fifteen big ones. Her insurance agent called. Thought it was odd she'd never filed a claim. Made my day.' The mole on his chin oozes blood. He wipes it with the back of his hand.

'Have you questioned her?' asks Hallinan.

'We busted her at her job. Dragged her out in cuffs. You should have seen the look on her boss's face.'

'You've got to be kidding,' says Tug. 'The woman's never had so much as a traffic ticket. If she knew the money was there she would have claimed it.'

'She was waiting until the heat was off. Listen, just because she has a clean driving record doesn't mean she didn't have her husband whacked.'

'That's suspicion, not evidence,' says Hallinan.

'Welcome to the twentieth century. We interrogated her for three hours, had her shaking in her pretty little shoes.'

'What did she say about the money?' says Tug.

'That she knew nothing about it. What do you think she'd say? We went at her with everything we had, but she wouldn't crack. I'll say this for her. Little as she is, she's got backbone.'

'Did you arrest her?' says Hallinan.

'We had to let her go, but this ain't the end of it.' Edwards wipes blood from his hand onto his pants. 'Wanna knock back a few brewskies?'

'Not today,' says Hallinan.

As Edwards walks away, Tug says, 'I'd

love to dump his ass in the tar pits with the other reptiles. He looks at Hallinan. 'Then again, what if he's right? What if she really did have her husband whacked?

When Hallinan gets home, he calls Amanda's apartment again and again, but there is no answer.

★   ★   ★

'I can't imagine who'd want those posters,' says the sheriff. Joe Bob Bell and Johnny Rafe Williams are already doing time, so it can't be for the reward.'

'What about the little girl missing out of L.A.?' says Stoneacre.

'Probably been dead from day one. That kind of case never ends well.'

'The kid looks vaguely familiar.'

'All them little blonde kids look alike.'

'Only three people were in here yesterday. Maggie Jones reported her cocker spaniel stolen. Hank Pitt reported a banged-up safe in the middle of Plummer Road. Ezekiel Bridger came in about the calves. I think I'll make a few inquiries on my way to Willow Shade. You wanna come?'

'No sense two men doing a one-man job,' he says, swinging his boots onto the desktop and adjusting the flow from the fan.

Ezekiel sees the deputy's car swimming through the heatwaves two or three miles down the road. He regrets reporting the stolen calves, but there's no taking it back. Bean is sitting bareback on Sunflower as Bear leads the pony through the shade at the edge of the corral. The heat is suffocating, a ring of sweat circling Ezekiel's hat band. He leans against the top rail.

'Hey, Bear,' he calls. She walks over, dragging the fat pony behind her. 'That'll be young Many Scalps about them calves. Why don't you take Bean inside so we men can have a private word?'

'I'll rub down the pony and . . . '

'Libra, I suggest you let that go for now.'

'But . . . ' Then it hits her. She looks at his grave expression. He knows. She sweeps Bean from the pony's back, removes the hackamore and rushes Bean inside.

Ezekiel is standing by the corral when Stoneacre pulls in. The car churns up a cloud of dust that powders the tops of his boots. 'Afternoon, Deputy Stoneacre,' he says. He extends his hand and they shake. 'I thought Amos would be riding shotgun today.'

Stoneacre smiles. 'Somebody has to jockey the fan.'

Ezekiel laughs. 'When you going to run for sheriff?'

'You think the county's ready for a half-breed on the ballot?'

'Far as I know there's only one woman remembers them scalps on your great-grandfather's lance and she's too old to make it to the polls. Any word on the Regan boy?'

'He's plenty busted up, but he'll live to ride another day.'

'Glad to hear he's going to make it. If you're ready to see them tracks we can take the pickup.'

'Let me get the casting mortar out of the trunk. A good set of tire tracks is as good as a fingerprint,' he says.

With the trunk of the car obscuring his face, Stoneacre takes a good look at the pony. There's a swath of sweat on his back where a small rider had been seated. He wouldn't have given it much thought if he hadn't stopped at the Last Chance on the way and talked with Millie.

14

Web of Secrets

Amanda's knees tremble as she climbs the stairs to her apartment. Dack is having a leisurely smoke on the walkway when she lifts the key from her purse. He is about to say something clever when he sees tears glittering in her eyelashes. She looks away and fumbles the key into the lock.

'You okay?' he asks.

'I can't talk right now, Dack.' She hurries inside, kicks off her shoes and drops onto the bed, finally giving in to her tears. She'll never forget the look on her boss's face when she was dragged off in handcuffs. No matter what she said to them, Conover and Edwards weren't interested in hearing the truth. The phone is ringing, but she's not up to talking to anyone right now.

After her interrogation, Edwards had

pushed her down the hall toward the exit. When no one was looking, he pinned her against the wall with a knee to her mid-section, jerked his head back and aimed directly at her face with his forehead. She let out a startled cry, but instead of head-butting her, he changed trajectory at the last second and drove his head into the wall. He winked at her, blood dripping from the mole on his chin. From a room down the hall a woman stopped typing and poked her head into the hall.

'Everything alright down there?' she asked.

'I stumbled,' said Edwards. 'Clumsy me.'

Amanda changes into slacks and sandals. She removes her pearl studs and drops them in her jewelry box. When she reaches for her bracelet, she notices three pearl studs instead of two. She stares at them. She can almost hear her heart beat in the quiet room. The third earring is an extra. It isn't hers. She hadn't lost it in Gavin's car, but someone had. Only one name comes to mind: Body Beautiful, Crystal Monet.

* * *

The phone is ringing when Hallinan walks in the front door. It's Tug. 'Meet me on Fairbanks,' he says. 'Someone at the house called for an ambulance. The coroner just arrived.'

'Jesus Christ!' says Hallinan.

'There's been a suicide.'

'Oh my god! Helen.'

When they arrive two coroner's assistants are carrying a covered body on a stretcher to the waiting van. Hallinan recognizes Jess Burnside, one of the attendants.

'What happened, Jess? I know these people.'

'It's Nathan Adler . . . you know . . . Plastic Surgeon To The Stars. He shot the family cat, then ate his gun.' Hallinan feels sick to his stomach.

'Mrs. Adler?'

'She's been asking for you. Her doctor's on the way.'

'I'll wait out front,' says Tug.

Mrs. Adler sits alone on the front room sofa. She holds out her hand. 'Lieutenant,

204

I knew you'd come.' Her voice is hoarse, her eyes red-rimmed. He sits beside her and holds her hand, so fragile and cold. 'I don't know what's gone wrong,' she says. 'This used to be such a happy house.'

'I'm so sorry, Helen. Tell me what happened?' She hands him a small folder. He lets go of her hand and unfolds it. 'A one-way ticket to Stockholm?'

'Nathan has been in touch with Sigrid all this time. She just kept leading him down the garden path. He called her this afternoon. Everything was fine until he said he was flying to Sweden. She finally confessed to having married months ago. Nathan dropped the phone and let out an anguished cry. I said, 'Nathan, you must pull yourself together.'

'He took a pistol out of the desk drawer. I said, 'Please, don't do anything foolish.' I followed him to the front balcony, pleading with him to be sensible. He shot Teddy. The cat let out a howl and tumbled into space. Then he turned to me with cold accusation in his eyes, like whatever had gone wrong was my fault. I thought he was going to shoot me, but instead . . . ' She shakes her head. 'It doesn't seem real.'

'He did all this to himself, Helen. None of it is your fault.'

Her doctor appears at the door, black bag in hand. He squeezes her hand and leaves. Media vans are pulling into the overlook. Hallinan can't believe how quickly bad news travels. He joins Tug at the bottom of the stairs. From the corner of his eye he sees movement in the star jasmine beside the garage. The sun has set and the purple shadows are deepening on the hillside. He kneels down. Two gold moons float among the foliage. He separates the branches, reaches out and gently touches the cat's head. Teddy growls softly. His left back leg is wet with blood. Hallinan removes his jacket and turns to Tug. 'Give me a hand? We have a survivor of this god-awful mess.'

When Hallinan leaves Fairbanks Drive and heads to his veterinarian's office, he never expects to see Mrs. Adler again. How wrong he is.

*   *   *

Amanda takes the Club Velvet card out of her jewelry box and dials the phone. A man picks up on the seventh ring.

'Club Velvet,' he shouts over the uproar in the background.

'Crystal Monet, please.'

'What?

'Crystal Monet,' she says, louder.

'Who's calling?'

Amanda thinks fast. 'It's about her Avon order.'

'Make it quick. She goes on in five minutes.' A fist pounds a wall.

'Yes, I've got it, Tom.' There's a click as he hangs up.

'Miss Monet, I think you may have lost a pearl stud earring in the car of a mutual friend,' says Amanda.

'Who is this?'

'Amanda Chase.'

She can hear the woman breathing on the other end.

'Three minutes to curtain!'

'I heard you the first time, Tom!' Then to Amanda: 'You waited a long time to call.'

'I'm calling now.'

'You can't call me here.'

'Where then?'

'Would you get your bony ass out here?' This time a different voice, deep and heavily accented.

'I'm coming, Cesar!'

'Can we meet for coffee?' says Amanda. 'Any place you say.'

'I'll get back to you. Don't call here again unless you want to get me killed.'

'Tell me something now? Anything I can hang onto.'

'I knew your husband, but I never slept with him.'

There's a click and she's gone.

Cesar. Amanda writes the name down.

⋆   ⋆   ⋆

Crystal looks in the mirror and asks herself if she'd been in love with Gavin or if she'd been using him. It's a complicated question. In her world, everyone uses everyone else.

⋆   ⋆   ⋆

Later that night Amanda wakes to the sound of rain. She lies staring into the shadows, unable to go back to sleep. She gets up and makes tea, watching rain drift through the eucalyptus grove across the road. She goes to the phone and dials Rusty's number. It's something she's wanted to do for the longest time. She yearns to hear his voice. She needs his reassuring touch and his strong shoulder to lean on. But what if a woman answers? What will she say? 'I know he's your husband, Mrs. Hallinan, but can I borrow him for the night . . . for a week . . . forever? You don't mind, do you?' She quickly hangs up. *Amanda, what are you thinking?*

* * *

Before Hallinan walks out the door of the veterinary clinic, he rests his hand on Teddy's head. Teddy looks up and purrs through his pain, as good a metaphor for life as Hallinan can think of. The bullet missed the bone and Dr. Butler has every confidence that he'll pull through.

He sits in the car and has a long slow smoke, leans his head on the back of the seat and watches rain-rivers slide down the windshield. His lower back is tight. His knee throbs with ghost pain. He coughs and cracks the window, then heads east on Santa Monica Blvd. to Vermont.

The Empire Hotel takes on a sorrowful aspect as night-rain drips from its rusty fire escapes and windowsills. Hallinan enters the lobby through the double doors of the recessed entry. Leather sofas and chairs flank tables covered with news-papers and magazines. Tropical plants sit beside old-fashioned pillars, and sand urns bristle with cigarette butts and dead matches.

The night clerk looks up and sets his racing form on the counter. The clock above his head reads 1:05. 'What can I do for you, officer?' he says. He's sixtyish with dyed black hair pomaded over his bald spot and a leaky pen in his shirt pocket.

'That obvious, Mr . . . ?'

'Parker Chitty. With that mug it's either L.A.P.D or the fire department, and the last time I looked the building wasn't on fire.'

'You're an observant fellow, Mr. Chitty. I'm here to do a welfare check on Miss Tyrisse Covington.'

'You're a week too late. You're the second officer been asking about her, but the other one was vice.'

'Stocky guy? Snout like a bulldog?'

'Complete with the snarl. I told him he was too damn short to be a cop. We didn't get along so good after that.'

Hallinan smiles. 'Storch has a twisted sense of humor.'

'Yup, that's the one. Storch. He tells me Miss Covington is a deadbeat and a trouble-maker and wants him out of here. Always says 'he' and 'him' just to be a jerk. I tell him he must be talking about another party, that our Miss Tyrisse is well-regarded. Storch looks the lobby up and down. The ceiling. The walls. Finally he says to me: 'You have a visit from the code inspector lately? I see three infractions just standing here.' Hell, the Empire is eighty years old. Once inspectors start poking around I might as well burn the damn place down. Nobody's got the money to bring these old buildings up to code.'

'So you asked her to leave.'

'I had to. I felt like a rat, but she kissed me on the cheek like a real lady. She asked me if she could leave a manila folder in the hotel safe for now and I said sure. She never even asked for her deposit back.'

'Any idea where she went?'

'Never saw her after that, but there's more to the story. Three days later Storch is back. He tells me to open the safe. When I refuse, he hits me on the side of the head with the butt of his gun, so I open it. I expect he wants money and jewelry. Instead he takes the manila envelope that belongs to Tyrisse and tells me to keep my mouth shut or else.'

'Did you ever look inside?'

'It was glued shut. I was curious, but I never opened it.'

'If you see her again, tell her to get in touch with Hallinan. She's a friend of mine.'

After he leaves the Empire, Hallinan

takes Sunset into the downtown. He stops in at Dark Desires, but the manager says he hasn't seen her in a couple of weeks. He cruises Main Street, the Waldorf and the donut shop on Main. He drives by Tyrisse's church, but it's dark except for the dim light above the rectory door. There's no sign of her or her car.

A transient shelters behind a row of trash cans. A stray dog shivers in the recessed entry of the cafeteria. If he can't find Tyrisse, maybe Storch can't either, unless he already has. Hallinan nods sleepily behind the wheel and heads for home, rain-shadows running like tears down his cheeks.

15

Out of the Midnight Rain

Hallinan is walking up the porch steps when he hears a car door open and close on the quiet street behind him. Against the far curb, a black car is parked in the darkness beneath a large oak tree. His hand moves unconsciously toward the gun in his shoulder holster.

A small figure steps into the pale halo of the streetlight, wearing a simple beige raincoat. She stands in a swirl of rain, the wind rippling the silk scarf at her collar, a glitter of raindrops beading her hair.

'Amanda!' he says, covering the distance between them at a jog. He puts his hands on her shoulders. 'Are you all right?'

'Not really,' she says, holding back tears. He pulls her close and she rests her forehead on his chest.

'Come inside,' he says. 'How long have

you been waiting out here?'

'I don't know. I fell asleep in the car.'

He lay her damp coat over a chair and leads her to the sofa. 'My God, your hands are like ice. I'll be right back.' He turns up the thermostat and goes into the kitchen, returning in a couple minutes with a cup of hot Ovaltine. 'Here, this will help warm you up.' He sits down beside her. 'I tried to reach you after I heard what Conover and Edwards put you through,' he says. 'Is that what you want to see me about?'

'No. Yes. I don't know.' Her hand trembles, rattling the cup against the saucer.

'It doesn't matter. I'm glad you're here.'

'I wanted to call you so many times, but . . . it was the wedding ring. I didn't want to impose . . . upset anyone.'

'Look,' he says, holding up his hand. 'The ring is gone. So is the woman who went with it.'

After a thoughtful pause, she says, 'I'm glad.'

'Me too.'

She smiles, setting her cup on the coffee table. He waits expectantly for her to speak, his eyes never leaving her face. 'I don't want to be alone tonight,' she says, meeting his gaze. 'My world is falling apart. I'm going under. I don't know how to cope with people like Conover and Edwards and I'm embarrassed to go back to my job. Mr. Cavendish has been good to me, but he'll fire me the minute I show my face.'

'I want you to stay here tonight, Amanda. We can talk about it tomorrow. I have a guestroom upstairs and something you can sleep in. I won't let you go under, I promise.'

Sometime before dawn, Amanda creeps silently into Rusty's room and slips in beside him. The summer rain ticks against the pane and wind blusters through the neighbor's wind chimes. Only half-waking, he wraps his arms around her and pulls her close. His embrace is like falling into a feathered safety net. She strokes his face. She kisses his cheek. He opens his eyes and begins to say something.

'It's all right,' she says and presses her mouth softly against his. 'Really, it's all right.'

Hallinan has plans to pick Amanda up after his shift. He wants to bring her to dinner at a place on La Cienega that serves big filets and drinks decorated with little paper umbrellas. He feels a hand on his shoulder as he approaches the exit of the stationhouse. When he turns around, he's looking into the flushed face of Marsh Edwards. His eyes are glazed, his breath incendiary.

'I saw you drop the Chase chick off at the Castleton this morning,' he says.

'Go home, Marsh. You're drunk.'

'You've got nerve, sticking your nose in my investigation.'

'You don't have an investigation. You have a vendetta. Now get the hell out of my face.'

'What's up with you? Don't tell me you're getting it on with that little tramp?'

Hallinan moves toward the door. Edwards blocks his path. Hallinan bumps him aside and keeps going, but Edwards grabs the shoulder of his suit coat from behind and hangs on.

Hallinan spins around faster than you'd think a big man could move, his elbow directed at Edwards' nose. The cartilage snaps like a dry twig. Edwards gives a sharp yelp and stumbles into the wall, blood dripping between his fingers as he holds the mismatched pieces of his face together. Breathing heavily, Hallinan straight-arms out the door without looking back.

Amanda is dressed in jeans, a blue-and-white-checked blouse and flip-flops when Hallinan arrives at her door.

'You've changed your mind about dinner,' he says.

'I'm too tired for anything fancy. Could we eat at your place?'

'Sure, but all I have are frozen TV dinners and half a bottle of cabernet.'

'Sounds like a real bacchanal. Why don't we eat on TV trays and watch *Dragnet*?'

'Sounds great to me.'

'By the way, Rusty, you have blood on the front of your shirt.'

He looks down. 'I wonder where that came from?'

Hallinan changes into something casual when they get to Sandalwood. He shows

218

off his fruit trees and flower beds, every-thing washed clean from the night's rain. Amanda kicks off her flip-flops. 'The grass feels so good,' she says. 'There's a small patch at the Castleton, but no one's allowed to walk on it.' She buries her nose in the sweet peas, the late-afternoon sun bring-ing out the gold highlights in her hair.

'How about an official guided tour of the house?'

She slips back into her flip-flops and they go up the porch steps. He holds the door and they go inside. 'Oh, this is wonderful,' she says, after she's seen every nook and cranny. 'I love a house that's been lived in, something with history.'

'There's three bedrooms, plenty of room for kids and . . . ' He cuts his words off mid-sentence. 'I'm sorry. That was insensitive.'

'Don't apologize. I've put the miscar-riage behind me. It wouldn't have been the best time to bring a child into the world. Once they catch the person who murdered Gavin, I'm closing the door on that chapter of my life.' She almost men-tions Crystal Monet and the man called

Cesar, but doesn't want to spoil the evening. She'll do some more information-gathering before she discusses it with anyone. 'Come on. Let's raid the refrigerator.'

16

Tragedy Strikes

There's a drum roll. Crystal steps into the spotlight. She wears a wig to cover her baldness, but the handful of feathers and rhinestones can't cover her skeletal frame. She's out of sync with the music and slowly peels off one long velvet glove. The footlights blur her vision. She stumbles and twists an ankle, but keeps smiling, tears running down her face.

Someone boos. She's no longer the fresh-faced healthy girl who danced to make money for nursing school. She's someone she doesn't recognize, someone who's lost her dreams and barely remembers what they were. A bottle smashes at her feet. A beer glass hits her shoulder. She stumbles into the wings and falls into the arms of old Tom. When she looks up, Cesar is staring at her, his face expressionless.

'You've got to get her to a hospital,' says Tom. 'This isn't right.'

'It's too late for that,' says Cesar. 'Put Ariceli on.'

★ ★ ★

'I'm going to grab a bite and stake out the Greyhound Station,' says Tug. 'A Nebraska woman says her sixteen-year-old son and his thirteen-year-old girlfriend are on their way to the city of broken dreams. You coming?'

'You go ahead. I'm picking up Teddy at the vet's and eating lunch at home.'

'You're not going to keep that fur ball?'

'I am.'

'You see Edwards in the coffee room?

'No. Why?'

'Looks like someone rearranged his face with a bar stool.'

'No kidding?'

'Yeah. He's got a broken nose, two black eyes and a cracked front tooth. He looks like the Frankenstein monster. I love it.'

'Maybe his girlfriend got tired of his

misogynistic bullshit.'

'There you go flaunting that Catholic school education again.'

'He hates women, Tug.'

'He hates everybody.'

'Everybody hates him.'

They're still laughing as Tug heads out the door.

Someone has dropped an envelope in Hallinan's in-box. It's from a deputy in Crazy Horse, California. He pulls out a cardboard backing and five grainy eight by ten photos, possibly taken through a telescopic lens. The deputy's card is enclosed with two words scribbled across the bottom: Daisy Adler?

A child riding a pony has been photographed from several angles. In the background is an old man and a woman with bushy red hair. If this is Daisy, how did she get from Griffith Park to Crazy Horse, hundreds of miles from where her clothes had been found? He compares the photos to the one on the missing person's flyer. Time has passed. It's hard to tell if they're of the same child. Before he talks to Helen, he wants to hear what the deputy has to say. He looks at the clock and leaves to pick up Teddy. He'll call the deputy after lunch.

Hallinan sets the cat carrier in the screened back porch behind the kitchen. He opens the carrier door, but Teddy hunkers toward the back, his eyes big and distrustful, his leg full of horsehair stitches. Hallinan leaves him to settle in with food, water, a new cat bed and a litter box, then goes to the kitchen and makes a sandwich. As he's getting settled, Tug calls.

'Rusty, turn on the news.'

'Why? What's happened?'

'You'll have to see for yourself, big guy,' he says, and hangs up.

Hallinan snaps on the TV. A reporter from an Arizona station stands in front of a vast landscape with a photogenic rock formation in the background. Behind the reporter is a movie set, a herd of cattle and horses, actors hugging one another and crying or sitting with their heads in their hands. Hallinan feels his stomach tighten and puts his sandwich aside.

'For those of you who are tuning in

late, I am reporting from the set of Dyna-mite Pass, outside Sedona, Arizona. This morning at ten o'clock, during a stampede scene, there was a tragic accident involv-ing popular cowboy star, Monty West. His horse's hooves became entangled in the lasso of another rider, plunging them both to the ground and crushing the popular young star beneath his mount. Head make-up artist and close friend, Dorothy Stanhope Hallinan, accompanied Mr. West by ambu-lance to the local hospital, where he was pronounced dead on arrival.'

'Geezus!' says Hallinan, thumping heavily into his chair. 'That poor kid.' His next thought is of Dorothy, but by the time he gets through to the hospital in Sedona, Dorothy has left.

* * *

Crystal lies shivering under a quilt in her dressing room. Tom brings her a bowl of soup and some crackers but she's too sick to eat. He's as scared of Cesar as she is, so when Cesar enters the room, Tom leaves. Cesar walks to the safe and removes the gun.

'Where are you going with that?' she says.

Without a word, he pockets the gun, closes the safe and spins the dial. Back in the hall he disables the pay phone. Later that evening, she hears him talking with his brother outside the dressing room. 'I've got to go out for a while, Fernando,' Cesar says. 'Keep an eye on Crystal. Make sure Tom keeps his hands out of the till, and have Ariceli hand over her tips.'

'What's the story with Crystal?'

'I'll be back later. We're driving to Riverside County. I think Tom needs to come too.'

'There's nothing out there except sand and buzzards.'

'Be a good brother. No more questions, okay?'

Five minutes later Crystal hears his car pull out of the lot.

17

The Big Uneasy

L.A. is a magnet for people in trouble, running from trouble or looking for trouble, and one doesn't have to look far in the general area of Main, Hill and Olive to find them. The one exception is Willie's Donut Shop, a peaceful oasis not far from Pershing Square where people gather after the clubs close down for the night. There are female impersonators, flamboyant night owls and miscellaneous personalities who defy precise definition even among themselves.

Tyrisse Covington, with her imperious cheekbones and androgynous sensuality, sits at a table with another highly successful female impersonator. Lady Precious lights their gold-tipped lavender cigarettes with a jeweled lighter from Cartier. A pink feather boa is tossed negligently over her silver-sequined gown. But instead of Mardi

Gras in *The Big Easy*, L.A. is Carnivale in *The Big Uneasy*.

Willie, in his scarlet beret, sees an unmarked and several black-and-whites fan out on the block. He's wary, but doesn't panic until Buzz Storch crawls by in his Studebaker, peering through the donut-shop window.

'Scatter!' cries Willie. 'It's a sweep.' Customers abandon their coffee cups and bump into tables as they pile out the back door, pulling off wigs, rubbing away lipstick, kicking off high heels to make better time in their stocking feet.

'I forgot my cigarettes,' says Tyrisse when she and Lady Precious reach the back door. 'I'll catch up.' In the seconds it takes to grab her smokes Precious is gone, both ends of the alley are blocked off, and two officers stand sentry out front. Willie kills the lights. They're trapped.

Tyrisse scribbles a number on a matchbook and hands it to Willie, who refuses to abandon his shop. 'Call Lieutenant Hallinan. Tell him to hurry. He needs to bring a gun and a camera, both loaded. I want everything on film this time.'

'You think he'll come?'

'Of course he'll come. He's my fiancé.' Tyrisse clips down the hall to the ladies' room, snaps off the overhead and locks herself in a stall. Willie crouches behind the counter and dials by the light of a match.

Storch sits in his car at the end of the alley, biding his time.

★   ★   ★

The phone rings as Hallinan heads out the door in his new tan slacks and Hawaiian shirt. He and Amanda have reservations at a restaurant on the coast that serves tropical drinks and clam chowder in bread bowls. If he answers it, it will be a solicitor. If he doesn't, it will be Amanda. Conflicted, he finally picks up.

'Hallinan here.'

'Rusty, this is Willie Camacho from the donut shop. Me and Miss Tyrisse are holed up here surrounded by cops. She says come with a gun and a camera. If Storch gets to us before you do, we'll be dead by the time you get here.'

Hallinan pauses for no more than three seconds. 'I'm on my way.' He dials Tug's number and explains the situation. 'I need back-up on this one.'

'I'm taking Linda to the Crescendo and you want me to get worked up about the oddballs at Willie's?'

Hallinan slams down the receiver and dials Amanda's number. After five rings, he hangs up. He bolts up the stairs, straps on his shoulder holster and grabs the Baby Brownie he used when he was camp counselor. He catches his reflection in the hall mirror as he heads out the door. He looks like a tourist from Iowa.

★ ★ ★

Amanda is in the shower when she hears the phone ring. By the time she picks up, the caller is gone. When she calls Hallinan there is no answer. She puts on her blue silk dress and sandals with starfish buckles and pulls her ponytail into a seashell barrette. Eight o'clock comes and goes. By ten she knows he isn't coming. It's beginning to feel like the night she waited for Gavin. When the phone finally rings she snatches it up.

'Rusty, where are you?'

'It's Crystal Monet. I'm in deep trouble, Amanda. If you pick me up, I'll tell you everything you want to know, but I have to get out of here . . . now.'

'Where are you?'

'In a phone booth outside Club Velvet.'

Amanda pens a hasty note for Rusty and tapes it to the door on her way out. Dack stands in the shadows at the end of the walkway. As soon as Amanda drives off, he reads the message she left for the fat cop. He runs for his car keys, always up for a little adventure.

* * *

Black-and-whites and unmarked cop cars are everywhere. Hallinan parks and shows his shield to a crew-cut grey-haired officer who's taped off the end of the access alley behind the Main Street businesses. He smiles when he sees the outline of Hallinan's gun.

'Go get 'em, boyo,' he says with a wink.

'They're guilty of congregating for immoral purposes.' Like drinking coffee and eating donuts? Or like the novitiates at St Joseph's Seminary? 'We'll clean this city up yet.'

To use the words 'city' and 'clean' in the same sentence is the Godzilla of oxymorons. They could start with Parker's racist and homophobic regime. Hallinan ducks beneath the yellow tape.

A paddy wagon is parked behind the all-night cafeteria next door to Willie's. Some of the occupants have mascara tears running down their cheeks. Others sport black eyes and expressions of self-righteous defiance. Most are trembling like puppies left out in the rain, and all are handcuffed like mass murderers. Tyrisse is not among them. 'Get 'em booked and printed,' says an officer, slamming the van door and waving the vehicle out of the alley.

Once the cops have had their fun, the black-and-whites thin out and Hallinan spots Storch's unoccupied Studebaker at the far end of the alley. The glass panel has been broken out of Willie's back door and unlocked from the inside. Hallinan cautiously enters the dark interior and

232

follows the back hall to the front eating area. It's dimly illuminated by the street light at the curb.

'Willie,' he whispers. 'It's Hallinan.'

A head rises from behind the counter, Willie's finger pointing down the side hall toward the ladies' room, where a wedge of light escapes beneath the door. There's a terrified cry and the sound of a metal waste receptacle clattering across the tile floor.

'I've got the photos.' It's Storch's voice, husky and menacing. 'The only thing left is the photo in your head and I'm going to blow it out your ears.'

Hallinan hears the sound of struggle, the ripping of material, a frightened shriek. He takes a few powerful strides and kicks the door in, ripping away a section of frame. The doorknob punches a hole in the wall behind it.

Storch stands in mute shock, the heavy buckle end of his belt ready to strike. Miss Tyrisse is cowering on her knees in front of him, her face battered, dress torn from neckline to waist, crystal beads from her necklace scattered across the floor.

Before Storch can react, Hallinan aims his camera and snaps a photo that catches him with his mouth open, his hand raised and his career in the toilet.

Storch reaches for the gun on the edge of the sink but it slips and clatters to the tile floor. When Rusty goes for his gun, his hand gets twisted in the folds of his Hawaiian shirt. So far, neither one of them is batting a thousand.

Tyrisse is curled in fetal position beneath the sink with her arms over her head. There's a mad scramble and Storch gets to his gun first. As Hallinan is deciding what homily he wants on his tombstone, Tug Boatwright blasts through the door, a serious-looking gun pointed at Storch's midsection.

'Drop it,' says Tug. Storch slowly lowers the gun.

Hallinan holds up his camera. 'When I tack this photo to the bulletin board in the muster room, you're going to be the most famous S and M star in Hollywood, especially with your brothers in blue. You think you can blow this one out of anybody's ears?'

The gun droops in Storch's hand as if it had become too heavy to hold.

'Drop it and hit the floor,' says Tug.

In one swift movement Storch shoves the gun in his mouth and pulls the trigger. The red-and-grey splatter that decorates the wall behind the urinals resembles a Jackson Pollock painting gone seriously awry.

18

The Dark Side of Town

When Hallinan reaches the Castleton, the BMW is gone from the lot and there's a note tacked to the door.

'Rusty, where were you? I've gone to pick up a woman named Crystal Monet at Club Velvet. She's going to tell me what happened to Gavin.'

Hallinan runs for his car. Club Velvet has gone by various names over the years, but its reputation is always the same: drugs, prostitution, gambling, loan sharking. Hardly a week goes by without a fistfight, cock-fight, knifing or sexual assault. He jams the gas pedal and the Buick flies over the asphalt as if it's been shot from a cannon.

★   ★   ★

It's the first time Amanda has crossed the Los Angeles River into Boyle Heights. In summer it's not much of a river, just an ugly concrete canal with a trickle of dingy water at the bottom. Every overpass and concrete wall she passes is plastered with gang graffiti. The recently constructed housing projects already show serious signs of indifference and neglect.

Amanda turns right on Clapton, a dirt road running through a tract of undeveloped land. A sign reading Dead End lies in the weeds. After a few hundred yards the road narrows and thick foliage closes in from both sides. She is so focused on the road that she's unaware of the vehicle following her at a casual distance.

Up ahead she sees the lights of Club Velvet, a purple stucco building with cracked ropes of neon looping beneath the sagging eaves. She doesn't know what to expect at the end of the road, so she decides to leave the car on the shoulder and approach the scene cautiously on foot.

★ ★ ★

Dack follows Amanda's car, separated by a tow truck, a Volkswagen and a church van. The Volks turns into a driveway and the van pulls up next to a storefront church. He follows Amanda across the river, sees her check the street signs and turn onto Clapton, the tow truck following at a crawl. Dack hangs back a few hundred yards. The next time he sees the BMW, the tow truck driver and his sidekick are hooking it to chains. Amanda is nowhere in sight. Dack stops and jumps out of the car.

'What the hell are you doing? I know the owner of this car.'

'If she doesn't make the payments she doesn't get to keep it,' says the bigger of the two big guys.

'I want to see some paperwork.'

'I have a copy of the pink slip. Come closer and I'll put it where the sun don't shine.'

The men are burly types with hairy arms, two against one. Dack decides to back off. Maybe he can turn the situation to his advantage. With her car gone Amanda is stranded. She'll have to depend on him to get back to civilization. Besides, he can't wait to get a look at the popular stripper. Maybe he'll get lucky. If not, he'll make his own luck.

* * *

Amanda stands behind an oak tree at the edge of the club's parking lot to get a feel for the place. A night wind ruffles her dress and she rubs her arms to stay warm. It's intermission. Men mill around the parking lot, smoking and drinking from bottles hidden in paper bags. There's a man in the phone booth where she's supposed to meet Crystal. There's a drum roll. A light above the entrance flashes and everyone except the man in the phone booth goes inside. She wants him to hurry so she can try Rusty's number again.

A hand touches her shoulder and she spins around with a gasp.

'Shh! It's just me,' says Dack.

'Dack! What the hell are you doing here? You almost scared me to death.'

'I read your note. Your car's been towed.'

'I don't believe you.'

'It's true. You should have made the payments.'

'Shut up, Dack! I want you to go. I can't think with you breathing down my neck.'

'If I leave, how will you get back?' He has a point.

'If you stay you have to help. When the man in the booth gets off the phone, call Detective Hallinan.' She recites the number. 'Tell him to get here as fast as he can. Then check the parking area for Crystal Monet while I check around back. You think you can do that?'

'Consider it done.'

Feeling less brave by the minute, Amanda walks down the side of the building past an overturned garbage can and follows a green light to the stage door. It's locked. She leans against the back of the building, cold and uncertain what she should do next.

Ten minutes later a man carrying a mop and bucket comes through the door and walks to his truck. Before the door closes she sticks her toe in the crack and steps inside. There are three doors opening onto the back hall. She opens the one with the gold star painted on the surface. Inside is a rack of costumes, a cluttered dressing table and a woman in a chenille robe lying motionless on a couch.

'Crystal?' she says. The woman's body is skin and bones, her closed eyes sunken hollows in a once-pretty face. Amanda shakes her gently. 'Crystal, it's Amanda Chase. I've come to take you out of this place.'

'It was cold outside. I had to come in.' Her voice is barely audible.

'It's all right. Have you been drugged?'

'No, I'm sick.'

'I'll help you up. You're going to the hospital.'

'We have to be out of here before Cesar gets back. He killed Gavin and he'll kill us too.'

'We can talk about that later.' She helps Crystal into her slippers. 'Lean against me. There, that's right.' Somewhere a door opens and cold air flows across Amanda's ankles. She holds her breath. Dack comes through the door and pauses when he sees the woman draped against Amanda's side.

'Did you reach Hallinan?'

'No. We can do this ourselves. Who's that?' he says. 'I thought we were here for Crystal Monet.'

'This is Crystal. Can you carry her? She weighs almost nothing.'

Dack backs away a step or two. 'That's Body Beautiful? She's bald as a baseball.'

'Damn it, Dack, give me a hand. We need to get her medical help. Someone's coming here to kill her.'

'To kill her! I didn't sign on for this bullshit.'

'It's not like I invited you here,' Amanda says angrily. 'Are you going to help or put your tail between your legs and run?'

'I wouldn't do that. I'll bring the car around.'

'Please, hurry!'

Dack flies out the door, tripping on the trash can as he races down the side of the building. He hits the road like a track star. When he gets to the car he leans forward, hands on knees, gasping for air, relief washing over him like a benediction.

He jumps behind the steering wheel, swings a tight u-turn and heads toward the main road. As he crosses the bridge he drifts over the center line and nearly sideswipes a blue-and-white car coming from the opposite direction. The driver swerves to avoid a collision and gives him the evil eye.

'Stupid greaser!' Dack yells. There's a loud bang and he ducks before realizing it's a backfire from the Mexican's car. He jams the gas pedal to the floor and rolls off the bridge to safety, nervous sweat popping in his armpits.

★　★　★

Amanda knows Dack has abandoned them. He's a coward, like every blowhard she's ever known. She guides Crystal to the exit. As her hand touches the doorknob an elderly man rushes toward them from down the hall.

'Tom,' says Crystal, her voice barely audible, 'help us.' He looks at them, then without speaking holds the door open to let them pass. He closes the door behind them and throws the deadbolt. Crystal moans and leans against Amanda's side.

They inch along the building to the trees across from the phone booth. Crystal collapses in the wet grass at the base of a tree. She's lost her slippers and the sash to her robe.

They hear a bang from the direction of the highway. 'That's Cesar's car,' says Crystal. 'I can't go any further.'

Cesar drives past their hiding place and parks behind the building. Amanda fishes a few dimes from the bottom of her purse. 'Stay here and don't come out. I'm calling for help.' She races to the pay phone. It dings as she drops a coin in the slot. She hears a car door slam and Cesar guns back down the driveway. He skids to a stop in front of the booth as the operator comes on the line.

'We need the police at 66620 Cl . . . ' Cesar jumps out of the car and rips the phone booth door open. A pane of glass tumbles onto the ground. '*Club Velvet!*' she screams into the phone. '*Club Velvet!*' He pulls the phone from the wall and jerks Amanda out by her hair. She's looking into dead eyes set in a face as pitted as the surface of the moon. He reminds her of a black scorpion, quick and lethal.

'Who the hell are you?' He backhands her across the face. Her barrette goes flying, his ring ripping through her hair. She screams in pain, her hair tumbling around her shoulders. He grabs her shoulder bag, pulls out the wallet and flips it open.

'Amanda Chase? I guess stupidity runs in the family. Where's Crystal?'

'Free.' A frightened whisper.

He scrapes a wooden match to life on his thumb nail, blows it out and jabs the fiery tip into Amanda's shoulder. It leaves a hole in her dress and an angry burn on her skin. She backs away with a sharp gasp and wraps her arms around her shoulders.

'Do you know what I'm going to do to that soft white skin of yours? By the time I'm through, you couldn't make your living as a two-dollar whore.' Amanda screams until he slaps it out of her. His eyes suddenly shift to a place beyond her shoulder and Amanda turns to see what he's looking at.

Crystal stands at the side of the road, her robe gone, her naked skin ghostlike in the moonlight. She doesn't seem to know where she is or what's happening. Cesar turns to Amanda. 'If you run I'll kill you,' he says dangerously. He throws her purse in the trunk of the car, then, without warning, cold-cocks her with a hard-knuckled punch to the jaw. He catches her as she falls and tosses her on top of her purse. He marches over, sweeps Crystal off the ground, throws her beside Amanda and slams the trunk.

19

Bullets and Blood

Hallinan's Buick goes airborne as he flies across the bridge. The car lands like a big cat on its muscular shocks. His heart thunders in his chest as he skids onto Clapton Road, his shirt snapping in the wind from the open window. He rumbles over the rutted road, keeping an eye out for Amanda's car, moonlight and shadows flashing over the Buick's polished hood.

A car comes toward him from the opposite direction, its beams on high. He shades his eyes against the glare as the blue-and-white Chevy flies by. He sees a trail of black smoke and smells oil burning off the head.

The car matches the description of the one at the scene of Gavin Chase's murder. Hallinan slams on his brakes, spins around and nearly goes over the steering wheel. When the Chevy turns right at the intersection, Hallinan is on its tail. He pulls parallel to get a look at the driver. He's a hard-looking character in a black cowboy hat.

Hallinan pulls his gun from the holster and sets it on the seat beside him, then holds up his shield and gestures for the driver to pull over. Instead, the man steps on the gas. Hallinan tosses his shield on the dash. At the next intersection, a young couple exiting a movie theater steps into the crosswalk. Hallinan lets the Chevy nose ahead of him a few feet, then taps the back left quadrant with the Buick's right front fender.

The Chevy fishtails, jumps the curb and tears a swath of grass from a residential lawn. Black Hat jumps from the car and whips a gun from his boot. Hallinan climbs from the Buick, his own gun in hand.

A bullet whines past Hallinan's ear, but before the man in black can pull off a second shot Hallinan takes careful aim, his first shot right on the money. The man drops his gun and falls to his knees. He needs both hands to plug the hole in his throat. He gulps a couple times, like he's trying to swallow the bullet, then falls face-forward and bleeds out on the grass.

By the time Hallinan takes the wallet from the dead man's pocket a crowd has gathered on the sidewalk. The driver's license is issued to Cesar Romero Navarro, age thirty-six: black hair, black eyes, black heart.

A plump, grandmotherly woman comes out of the house in her robe and curlers. The back end of the Chevy has come to rest in her rose bush, the trunk having sprung open on impact. She looks inside, then begins waving her arms and firing off reels of tommy-gun Spanish. Hallinan rushes over. Two women lie motionless in the trunk. One of them is Amanda.

★　★　★

Amanda regains consciousness in the ambulance, reaching across the aisle to the other stretcher and squeezing Crystal's hand. There is a weak response. As they fly through the streets with sirens wailing, the police swarm Club Velvet. They arrest a dozen men on bench warrants, drug possession and illegal weapons charges. As soon as Hallinan turns the scene of the shooting over to Hollenbeck Division he races to the hospital.

* * *

Although battered and bruised, Amanda waives medical treatment so she can stand with Hallinan, a doctor, and a chaplain and witness Crystal's dying declaration. As she finishes her narrative, Crystal's breathing becomes shallow and her eyes drift shut. The doctor feels for a pulse. She's gone. He pulls the sheet over her face.

'What was wrong with her?' asks Amanda. 'Why was she so emaciated?'

'Her liver is badly distended. I think the autopsy will show that her uterine cancer metastasized to vital organs. If she'd had treatment in the beginning, she might have had a fighting chance.' He turns to Amanda. 'Is there someone who can stay with you tonight?'

Hallinan puts his arm over her shoulder. 'She's coming home . . . with me.'

★ ★ ★

'At least I know now that they met at Dr. Fraley's Clinic,' says Amanda after she and Hallinan are tucked in for the night. 'I wonder why Gavin confided in her and not me about his cancer.'

'He didn't want to worry you. He'd have told you eventually, or you'd have figured it out on your own.'

'I found her business card in Gavin's car. Crystal said they had a phone relationship. There had to be more to it than that.'

'You'll never know. The players are off the stage. The theater's gone dark.'

'I didn't realize you were so poetic.' She gives him a kiss on the cheek. 'I'm not going to obsess over it, but I still wonder why he took the station wagon instead of the BMW that night.'

'Listen, if I drove into Boyle Heights on New Year's Eve, I'd drive the oldest wreck

I had.' Amanda yawns and snuggles deeper into his shoulder. 'Stay in bed in the morning. Let me take care of you.'

'I don't want to wear out my welcome.'

'You don't understand. I love you. I want to take care of you forever. I come with a house, a cat and a garden. What more can a girl want? Marry me, Amanda. Please.'

★   ★   ★

Helen looks out on the wooded hill behind the house. Hallinan recalls the day they sat here watching the rain beat against the pane, Helen looking red-eyed but composed in her jade lounging pajamas. Today he sits in the chair beside her bed.

'Good to see you, Hallinan.'

'How are you, Helen?'

'Oh, I'm okay, I guess. I seldom leave the bed these days. The doctor says it's kidney failure. I guess you saw the For Sale sign out front. It's hard parting with the house, but time marches on. So what's in the envelope? My cat? It's all right. I imagine you did the right thing and put the poor fellow out of his misery.'

'No, I took him to my vet. He'll be good as new when the stitches come out.'

'Well, that's good news. Just don't bring him back here,' she says with a laugh. 'Sarah has all she can handle. Now, why don't you tell me why you're here?'

'I received a few photos from a deputy sheriff out by the Mojave. He thinks a child living on a nearby ranch resembles your daughter.'

'Wishful thinking, I fear, but I'll take a look.' She puts on her bifocals and looks carefully at each photo. Hallinan waits quietly. 'I'll call you in a day or two. I need more time with these photos,' she says.

20

Revelation

When Hallinan returns home that evening, the bed is made and Amanda is gone. The note pinned to the pillow says: 'In answer to your question: yes. You're stuck with me now. I've gone back to the apartment to start packing my things. Amanda.'

Hallinan is humming happily, coffee perking on the stove and the fixings of a shrimp salad on the counter, when there's a knock at the door. The kitchen clock reads nine. He opens it, expecting to see the paperboy coming to collect.

'Dorothy!' She's wearing a tailored black sheath with a wide white belt and strands of red beads, looking even thinner than the last time he'd seen her.

'I lost my key,' she says, pushing past him with Beezer in the crook of her arm and a suitcase in hand. She sets the suitcase inside the door and lowers the dog to the floor. He wears a fringed vest and a little red cowboy hat and goes straight to the site of his former food bowl before Hallinan can stop him. There's a sharp yelp of surprise as he flies back into the front room, his hat cocked to one side, his toenails sliding on the hardwood floor.

'Sorry, Beezer,' he says. 'That's your new brother, Teddy.'

Teddy stands in the doorway between the kitchen and dining room, his back arched, his ears back, his fur puffed up like a Halloween cat. Dorothy sits on the sofa by the fireplace and Beezer jumps trembling into her lap.

'I see you've found a replacement for Beezer,' she said.

'He needed a home and I had one to offer. You look frazzled. Let me get you a cup of coffee.' He goes to the kitchen and returns with two steaming cups. He sets hers on the coffee table and settles across from her in his easy chair.

'How are you, Dorothy? I tried to reach you when I heard about Monty.'

She kicks off her high heels and rubs her swollen toes. 'I'm the beneficiary on

Monty's life insurance policy,' she says. 'His parents are furious. Can you believe they're going to take me to court? It seems word of my existence never reached the wilds of Montana.'

'Wyoming, Dorothy. Monty was from Wyoming.'

'Whatever,' she says. She taps a cigarette from her pack. Hallinan does not jump up. She fishes matches from her purse and lights it.

'As you see, I came with suitcase in hand. I need a place to stay while I make plans. I'm thinking France. The best cinema is out of Europe these days.' Beezer blinks at the smoke coming off the tip of her cigarette.

Hallinan looks at her over his cup and takes a thoughtful sip. 'I don't think that's a good idea, Dorothy.'

'Europe?' she says, blowing the steam from her cup.

'No. Coming here.'

She sets her cup down with a click. 'You've met someone,' she says.

'I have.'

'Do you want to tell me about her?'

'I don't.'

'Was she also a stray?' Hallinan does not take the bait. 'Sorry, I shouldn't have said that. Have you slept with her?'

'I'm in love with her.'

'That's a big gamble at your stage of life.'

'It's all a gamble, Dorothy. Maybe this time the odds are in my favor. Since you're here, I want you to level with me. Where did we go wrong? Was it losing the baby? My long hours? What?'

She leans back, takes a drag from her cigarette and blows the smoke toward the ceiling, then leans forward with an elbow on the knee of her crossed legs.

'For a cop you've got a real blind spot, Rusty.'

'Would you care to elaborate?'

'I hustled you into marriage. I'm surprised you never figured that out. I didn't get pregnant on our honeymoon. I was pregnant when I walked down the aisle in that stupid white gown.'

'But we never . . . '

'No, we never,' she says. 'So, why you and not him — ? He was married, but not so married he didn't like having a young girl on the side. He wouldn't give me money to . . . you know . . . get rid of it. When I miscarried, I was delighted. Delighted! I had ambitions. There was no room for a child in my plans. I couldn't think of a graceful exit strategy from the marriage, so I toughed it out. There you have it.'

There was a time when this information would have had a crushing effect, but Hallinan feels neither anguish nor outrage, just a sense of relief as the last psychological shackle that binds him to Dorothy falls away.

He sets his cup down and walks to the dining-room table, returns with the legal papers and hands them to Dorothy. 'Signed and sealed, just like you wanted. My only request is that you go to Vegas and get it done yesterday, if not sooner.'

Hallinan walks over and lifts Beezer's chin with a finger. Beezer thumps his tail and gives him a questioning look. Hallinan straightens his little red hat. 'There you go,' he says. 'Now you're a real cowboy.'

He looks at Dorothy. 'I want you to go now.'

* * *

Hallinan puts in a call to Crazy Horse and gets Deputy Stoneacre on the line. After a few pleasantries Stoneacre says, 'The elderly man in the photo is Ezekiel Bridger. I've always known him to be an upstanding citizen. The red-haired woman, Libra Gordy, recently inherited the ranch where the photos were taken. She has no record, but as a teenager she spent time in a sanitarium for depression and delusional thinking.'

'What kind of delusions?'

'The head physician at Sunny Oaks says Miss Gordy believes the Catholic Church stole and sold her newborn. The home for unwed mothers denies she's ever been in residence.'

'That's some story.'

'Her stepfather told her therapist that she'd never been pregnant, that the girl has always been a little off. Now, here's the zinger. Miss Gordy was in the Los Angeles area at the time Daisy Adler disappeared.'

'You've certainly done your homework, Deputy. Let me catch up on my end and

I'll get back to you,' he says, ending the call.

'Are those the photos from the donut shop?' asks Tug when Hallinan is off the line. He points to the yellow packet on the corner of Hallinan's desk.

'That's it. Go ahead and open them. Tug rips the packet open and flips through the photos. He bursts out laughing.

'The drugstore gave you the wrong ones, big guy.'

'What?' says Hallinan.

'A boy in a canoe? A watermelon-eating contest? A kid shooting an arrow at a bale of hay?'

'Let me see those,' says Hallinan. Tug passes them over. He looks at the photos and can't stop laughing. 'I took those when I was camp counselor. I thought I had new film in that camera.'

'You mean Storch blew his brains out for nothing?'

Hallinan gives him a sly look. 'I wouldn't go that far.'

The phone rings and Hallinan picks up. 'Yes, Helen. Okay. Sure. I'll be there in twenty minutes.'

'Oh no,' says Tug. 'I'm meeting Linda for lunch. Helen Adler is all yours.'

★ ★ ★

Helen answers the door in a white summer dress and a necklace of Italian glass beads. She looks fragile and slightly stooped, but something is different in her demeanor, like a dark cloud has lifted.

The drapes are open and sunlight floods the front room, a dozen potted geraniums blooming on the balcony. She invites Hallinan into the den and they sit across from one another at the desk.

'I have something to tell you,' she says.

'Is this about the photos?' he asks. 'Did you recognize the child?'

'I recognized both of them, Lieutenant.'

'Both of who?'

'Daisy and the woman with the red hair.'

'Are you sure? The woman has a history of mental illness. Delusions. I have that on good authority.'

Helen smiles. 'They aren't delusions.'

'I'm confused. What are you talking about?'

'Years ago Nathan and I took an extended vacation and returned with a newborn baby. Daisy. We said she was ours. We were lying. The Catholic Church helped us adopt from the Home for Delinquent and Wayward Girls.'

'You're Jewish. The church doesn't sanction adoptions outside the faith.'

'Don't be naïve, Hallinan. Money talks. Our overnight conversion was nothing short of miraculous. I couldn't recite the rosary if you held a gun to my head. Libra Gordy was a kid back then. A lot of the girls at the Home couldn't wait to get rid of their babies so they could go to the senior prom, get on with their lives and pretend nothing ever happened. Libra Gordy was stubborn and bright. She fought to keep her baby. I admired her for that.

'One day we were called to the convent and told they had a baby for us, that the mother had died in childbirth. That mother was Libra Gordy. She was probably told that her baby had died. As you see, they are both very much alive.'

'I don't get it. How did she end up with Daisy?'

'I have no idea. Maybe she uncovered records. Maybe it was divine providence if you believe that sort of thing. I knew there was something off from the beginning, but it was easier to lie to myself. The whole operation was riddled with corruption.'

'Helen, you've really put me on the spot here. You know I can't pretend this conversation never happened.'

'And you don't have to. I'm not going to be around much longer, but I intend to set things right before I go. I want to see Daisy one last time and I need your help.'

★ ★ ★

After several phone conversations between Hallinan, Deputy Stoneacre, Helen's lawyer, Shmulie Braverman, and Libra Gordy, a meeting is scheduled to take place at Willow Shade. It's a sweltering day in Hollywood and it only gets hotter as they drive into the Mojave. Everyone is on edge.

On the last leg of the trip the heat crackles like a furnace. Hallinan can smell the asphalt melting under the tires as he follows Deputy Stoneacre's car deep into the heart of the Mojave. Everyone is dressed lightly except Shmulie in his black suit, his dark hair curling around his yarmulke, his nose buried in documents. He looks like a pubescent yeshiva student — thin, pale, and studiously myopic in his Coke-bottle glasses.

The landscape flies by — endless miles of sand, cactus, and the occasional miner's shack. A herd of wild burros wanders along the horizon. There's an austere beauty in the place, but all Hallinan can think about is a cool, dark bar and a tall, frosty mug of Guinness.

The turn signal flashes on the patrol car ahead of them. A broad, shallow creek flanked by a wide band of wild grass and willow trees comes into view. A couple dozen head of mixed-breed cattle graze in the shade. They follow Stoneacre's car into the driveway and pass a rock garden and corral before parking in front of the house.

Hallinan looks at Helen. 'You going to be okay?'

'I think so,' she says.

'Stay put. I'll be right back.'

Stoneacre and Hallinan get out first. Ezekiel Bridger exits the barn with a hound at his heels. There are introductions and handshakes. 'I figured you were on to us the last time you came out, Stoneacre,' says Bridger. 'Miss Gordy and I have had several conversations regarding her daughter. We just don't want any emotional displays in front of the child.' Hallinan motions to Helen. Shmulie helps her out of the car.

Libra Gordy steps onto the porch, a sturdy, handsome woman, comfortable in her surroundings. Her hair is gathered off her neck like a sheaf of flaming wheat. She wears a yellow T-shirt, jeans and tennis shoes. The child at her side has a gingerbread tan and shoulder-length braids . . . a slimmer, taller version of the Daisy Adler on the poster. When she looks at Helen there's no sign of recognition, whether real or by design.

'Why don't you come inside,' says Libra. 'I have a jug of lemonade in the ice box.' As they move up the steps, the dog crawls into the shade under the house.

'You go on in, Shmulie,' says Helen. 'I

have no patience for legal mumbo-jumbo.'

Daisy laughs. 'Mumbo-jumbo! That's a funny word. Do you want to see my kittens? They're up in the loft.'

'I don't think the lady is dressed for climbing in hay lofts,' says Libra. 'Why don't you let her catch her breath.'

'I'll be fine,' says Helen. 'I can stand in the shade while she shows me the horses.'

'I'll bring you some lemonade. Go ahead, Bean. Show her how you ride bareback on Sunflower.'

'Thank you. I would like that very much,' says Helen.

In the space of an hour the initial process of legally reuniting Daisy Adler with her biological mother has begun. The visitors return to their vehicles. Schmulie is already talking about initiating an investigation of the Home for Delinquent and Wayward Girls.

Daisy runs up to Helen, who's in the back seat of the Buick. She wraps her arms around Helen's neck. 'I know that perfume,' says the child. 'The bottle sat on a vanity by a window. It's Windsong.' Helen gives her a squeeze.

'Yes, darling, it's Windsong. You take good care of that nice pony now. You're a lucky little girl . . . Bean.'

As Hallinan walks past the rock garden with Ezekiel, he looks down at the license plates propped among the rocks. One in particular catches his eye.

'Mr. Bridger, would you consider selling me that 1952 plate?'

'You can have it. It's nothing special.'

'Thank you, sir. Do you remember how you came by it?'

'I found it about three years ago out by Buzzard Lake.'

'Do people go out there to fish?'

'Nobody local. There ain't been water in it since the time of the dinosaurs.'

'Any abandoned vehicles out that way?'

'I see an old hulk from time to time, but mostly I'm looking for rattlesnakes.'

As they drive away, Daisy waves from the porch, then turns and goes inside.

⋆　⋆　⋆

The night is dark and blustery, the warm Santa Ana winds sweeping off the desert

267

and swirling the candle flames in the pumpkins on Rusty Hallinan's front porch. Teddy watches curiously from the window as he drops generous handfuls of candy in the trick-or-treat bags. He hears Amanda setting the table and smells the pot roast and pumpkin pie through the screen door.

When the last of the trick-or-treaters had come and gone, Hallinan settles in the porch swing and studies the license plate from Willow Shade. It belonged to the truck his father had been driving when his parents vanished. He squeaks lazily back and forth, letting his mind drift with the purple smoke from his cigarette. He needs to retrace his parents' route as they drove through the Mojave toward Nevada. He wants to know where they stopped for gas, who spoke with them, whose memories go back six years. He considers turning in his badge and doing private investigations before his knee gives out again.

The wind comes up and leaves cartwheel across the lawn. A few days ago he drove by the pink house. The For Sale sign was down, an unfamiliar car parked in the garage. He stood at the overlook with the Hollywood sign to his left, the observatory across the hills to the east. In his hand was the evening paper containing the obituary of Helen Adler, a woman who would always occupy a poignant corner of his psyche. He'd been here on the night Daisy went missing and played it out to its unlikely resolution on a desert ranch called Willow Shade. He'd lingered a while longer with his memories, then driven back down the hill toward Hollywood Blvd.

Hallinan looks up as a black limousine rolls to a stop behind his Buick. The passenger door opens and closes. A tall silhouette in spike heels clicks up the steps to the porch. Tyrisse Covington materializes in a snug gold lamé dress and an arsenal of jingling glitz. She looks like a million bucks. Okay, a million counterfeit bucks. Hallinan pulls himself up, his knee giving an ominous pop.

'Rusty, my love, I couldn't leave without saying goodbye. Lady Precious and I have worked up an act. We're opening in Vegas next week. Move over Sammy Davis, Jr.'

'That's great, Ty. You'll knock 'em dead.' Does she really have a Vegas booking? With Ty you can never be sure.

'Are you going to leave without telling me about the photo?'

'When I was camera girl at Dark Desires, an up-and-coming politician wanted his picture taken with a pretty blonde impersonator on his lap. He was already on the ballot, wanted to do a lot of good things for the city. He was in a long-term marriage, but he also had some gender identity issues to work through.

'It wasn't until I'd snapped his photo that I realized I'd captured Storch in the background. He was pocketing his weekly protection money. I hadn't known he was there until our eyes met. He was apoplectic, determined to get his hands on that camera.

'Luckily, the place was jumping. By the time he elbowed through the crowd, the politician and I were out the back door. We were two blocks away in his Lincoln when the photo popped out of the Polaroid. We couldn't stop laughing.

'In Storch's hands it would have been

the money shot of the year. He'd have cropped himself out of the picture and either sold the politician's image to *L.A. Confidential* or blackmailed him.'

'You could have destroyed it.'

'Storch knew too much. I needed something equally scandalous on him to keep him from exposing the politician.'

'That's some story, Ty.'

'The politician won the election, his wife at his side, everything peachy-keen. He never came back to Dark Desires and I never saw him again, except on TV.'

Tyrisse glances through the screen door. Amanda is taking the roast from the oven. 'Now that you're married to that pregnant woman, I suppose we'll have to call off our engagement, although it wounds me deeply to do so,' she says.

'Why don't you and Miss Precious have dinner with us? We'd love to have you.'

'Wish I could, but we've got to hit the road.'

'I'll miss you, partner. We put a lot of bad guys away. Promise you'll take care of yourself. No swimming in the deep end of the pool.'

She pulls a bottle of expensive brandy from her purse and hands it to Hallinan. 'A parting gift,' she says. 'We'll never have Paris, darling, but we'll always have the ladies' room at Willie's Donut Shop.'

THE END

Other titles in the
Linford Mystery Library:

THE WHITE LILY MURDER

Victor Rousseau

When New York department store magnate Cyrus Embrich is found stabbed to death at his office desk, the police have little evidence to go on. Embrich's secretary reveals that her employer had been in fear of his life, and in the event of anything happening to him, he had asked her to call in the famed private investigator 'Probability' Jones to assist the police. Aided — and at times led — by his able assistant Rosanna Beach, Jones finds himself caught up in the most complex and dangerous case of his career . . .